Critical acclaim for

Richard Grayson's earlier books:

"Grayson shows a sense of humor and appreciation of the weird. This writer is not afraid to take risks, and he can be very funny indeed...A versatile, interesting experimenter... Grayson knows New York City, where many of his stories are set, inside and out... Compulsively talky and engagingly disjunctive."
– *Publishers Weekly*

"The incessant familiarity of the writer's secret self makes his world entertaining and bizarre. The dialogue is consistently, even ingeniously funny... bright and keenly made."
– *The New York Times Book Review*

"Grayson is a born storyteller and standup talker. Highly recommended." – *Library Journal*

"An underground post-modernist who writes comic fiction crammed with details adopted from pop culture and the daily news...capable of less self-conscious, more serious (though not less comic) work." – *Kirkus Reviews*

"Grayson is shaking funny ingredients together like dice." – *Los Angeles Times*

"Convulsively inventive...The reader is dazzled by the swift, witty goings-on." – *Newsday*

"Where avant-garde fiction goes when it turns into stand-up comedy." – *Rolling Stone*

"Grayson has a splendid command of language; he is steeped in literary history, is highly inventive."
– *Orlando Sentinel*

"Grayson is able to create a full range of masks behind which the artist peers out to make his criticisms of modern life. Among writers born in the mid-point of our century, he holds an important spot." – *Israel Today*

"Slices of life as we know it right here and now...funny, intelligently written and original. These stories accurately capture snapshots of our culture at a very interesting moment."
– *South Florida Sun-Sentinel*

"A satirist and parodist so timely that his brothers and sisters may not yet discern themselves in his mirror... Clearly a master of the genre...Wherever Grayson casts his gaze, he manages to isolate panoramas of city and small town life in America from the 60s to the present." – *American Book Review*

"This is very funny stuff... Richard Grayson has a fresh, funny voice." – *Philadelphia Inquirer*

"An audacious and wickedly smart comedic writer... An iconoclast sways to his own beat, making beautiful music along the way." – *Kirkus Discoveries*

WHO WILL KISS THE PIG?

SEX STORIES FOR TEENS

RICHARD GRAYSON

Dumbo Books ◊ Brooklyn 2008

These stories originally appeared, in somewhat different form, in the following literary magazines and webzines: *California Quarterly, Washington Review of the Arts, Brooklyn Literary Review, New Writers, City, Three Sisters, Westerly Review, Browns Mills Review, Hanging Loose, Blithe House Quarterly, Avery: An Anthology of New Fiction, Fifth Sun, Maelstrom Review, Bellingham Review, Telescope, Unfinished Stories, Twaddle, Fiction Warehouse, Spillway Review, Pindeldyboz, Six Little Things* and *3:AM Magazine*.

Printed in the United States of America.

Dumbo Books, 72 Conselyea Street, Brooklyn, New York 11211

E-mail: dumbobooks@yahoo.com, Richard.Grayson@yahoo.com

First Edition

ISBN 978-0-6152-0547-2

10 9 8 7 6 5 4 3 2 1

For my brothers,

Marc and Jonathan

CONTENTS

WHO WILL KISS THE PIG?

SEX STORIES FOR TEENS

Who Will Kiss the Pig?

Seated near a table in the law school atrium, Professor Dash gingerly took hold of the piglet that Yassir handed him.

The previous two weeks, the table had held thirty plastic piggy banks, each labeled with the name of a professor, as students from the Public Interest Law Society sat by a sign saying WHO WILL KISS THE PIG?

Each night Yassir compiled a running total of the money law students placed in the various piggy banks and emailed it to ALLSTU and ALLSTAFF.

Professor Dash, known as "D+ Dash" for his notoriously low grades in Civil Procedure, did not seem to be in the running at first, but on the second Wednesday someone had placed a twenty-dollar bill in his piggy bank, and after that, his lead only increased. Yassir, a third-year student, heard that essays answering a practice final exam question on personal jurisdiction had been returned that Tuesday.

Yassir had borrowed the pig from the admissions director's mother and had passed on the woman's warning that Beth-Ann sometimes got startled when humans made abrupt moves. As about forty law students, staff members and the school's director of facilities looked on, Yassir said it was time to proceed with the kiss. It didn't have to be on the pig's moist snout.

Slowly Professor Dash lowered his head and touched his lips to Beth-Ann's forehead.

It reminded him of an impulsive gesture he'd once made following an encounter with a Boston boy with heavily moussed hair.

This Person Is Already Your Friend

Diego blamed Miranda for getting his medical license suspended, so he married Miranda's mother and tried to humiliate Miranda by replacing Miranda's father's portrait with one of himself.

After Miranda's mother died, Diego decided to become friendly with Miranda's husband and learned he had a brain tumor he was keeping a secret from Miranda. Diego lied to him and said that the brain tumor was causing blackouts during which he became violent, finally convincing the husband to leave Miranda for her own good.

Then Diego framed Miranda for embezzlement and seduced Miranda's teenage son.

A few years later, Miranda learned about the existence of Diego's half-brother Kevin and married him. For a while Diego pretended to be friendly with the couple, but he had a plan. He lured Kevin to a ski spa in Vermont by phoning him and telling him that Miranda had broken her leg and needed him. Kevin arrived only to find his wife and another woman together in bed. That ended Miranda's second marriage.

Miranda and the woman moved in together, infuriating Diego. He decided to seduce the young man who worked as Miranda's assistant. But Diego fell in love with him, and they were very happy for a while.

However, when the young man died in a plane crash, Diego blamed Miranda for sending him on the fatal business trip in her place. So he persuaded a young college student to file sexual harassment charges against Miranda's partner, a professor of women's studies.

In retaliation, Miranda stuffed Diego into a trunk and moved him to a secret coal cellar, holding him captive for weeks. After she finally released him, Diego did something out of character. He said they were even and vowed to make amends with Miranda.

Unfortunately, on his way to Miranda's office to donate money to her pet charity, a foundation to help agoraphobic children, Diego accidentally ran down Miranda's pregnant daughter-in-law and caused her to lose her baby and almost her life.

Although it took many months for Miranda to forgive Diego for killing her grandson, eventually they buried the hatchet. When Diego confided to her that he was dying of prostate cancer, Miranda arranged for him to go to Latvia for experimental treatments.

How to Become an Excitable Nun

When it comes to nuns, I am a man of limited experience.

Although I grew up two blocks away from a small convent, I was not Catholic and spent my childhood merely saying, "Hello, Sister," when one of the black-habited nuns would cross my path. Some of them were cheerful, some more severe, but not one of them seemed particularly excitable.

The first nun I got to know fairly well was a fellow student in a graduate class in the history of English and the Romance languages. She was not at all excitable. I know this because one night Professor Jochnowitz was discussing the origins of vulgar words and I raised my hand and asked, "Where does the word *cunt* come from?" My classmate the nun did not even raise an eyebrow and she was perfectly friendly to me after that question, a question to which I have long ago forgotten the answer.

But a decade later, I was a college professor myself, and I was taking another graduate class trying to learn computer programming. It was the early 1980s and it was believed that all of us would have to learn computer programming in order to create exams and lesson plans and to do administrative tasks in higher education.

At the Apple II+ computer next to me was another nun, a dean at a local Catholic women's college. The president of her college made her take this computer programming course and she did not want to do it. She was an excitable nun.

I learned how excitable she was when the students were paired off for their final projects. She and I were partners and whenever we would find a bug in the program we were writing, this nun would very loudly say, "Oh, shit!"

Because we were novices with the Basic programming language, and because no matter what Steve Jobs will tell you, the Apple II computer was not reliable, there were lots of setbacks during the weeks this nun and I met to complete our class project. And she constantly yelled – *yelled* is not too strong a word – "Oh, shit!" I think if she were not a nun – she did not wear a habit, only a plain black dress and a large silver cross – the computer lab coordinators would have tried to silence her.

Finally, the project was done and our computer program ran – not flawlessly, but good enough to turn in for a grade. To celebrate our project's completion, I told the excitable nun I would treat her to a cup of coffee at the Greek diner across from the computer lab.

She ordered tea, but our waitress brought us two coffees.

"Didn't you hear what I ordered?" the nun yelled at the waitress. "What's wrong with you?"

I felt I knew her well enough now to ask her the question.

~ 6 ~

"Sister Mary Barbara," I said, "how did you become so excitable?"

Her green eyes flashed with fury.

"Guess!" she snapped.

Unfortunately, I have a limited imagination.

Hey Jude

There once was a woman who was assistant dean of student affairs at a fourth-tier law school. In her freshman year of college, this woman's favorite class was English 2.2, Introduction to Fiction. Her instructor had the class read many books she loved, including Hardy's *Jude the Obscure*. She was the only student who raised her hand when the instructor asked the class the meaning of the book's epigraph, "The letter killeth."

"I think it means 'the letter of the law,'" the girl who would become assistant dean of student affairs at a fourth-tier law school had said back then. "That's what really messed up Jude and Sue's lives so much."

This woman's life was not as messed up as those of Jude Fawley and Sue Bridehead.

Her biggest disappointment was that after getting a Ph.D. in English, she could not secure a full-time job as a literature professor. After years of scraping by as an adjunct lecturer teaching composition and remedial writing, she decided to go to law school and eventually ended up as a law school administrator.

Sometimes she took a special interest in certain students. For example, there was one student she kept a close eye on because he reminded her of her only nephew: the young man had the same first name as her nephew and was the only South Asian male in his first-year class. (Her nephew had been born in India and adopted.)

This student did not get good grades his first year. In fact, at the end of the academic year, his grade point average was below 2.0 and he was on academic probation. But because the student had recently moved and had not given his new address to the law school, the letter about academic probation sent in May never reached him.

It was only in late November of this student's second year, just before final exams, that he was surprised to learn that he was on academic probation. He had come in to see the assistant dean about another matter entirely.

The assistant dean of students told him that he needed to get his grade point average up to 2.0 by the end of the spring semester or he would be academically dismissed after spending a lot of hard work and over $60,000 on two years of his legal education. Then she said, "You're not an officer of any student organization, are you?"

The student said, yes, he was vice president of the Asian Pacific American Law Students Association. The assistant dean just nodded.

Her supervisor, the associate dean, had told her to report anyone on academic probation who was violating the rule against such students being an officer of an organization.

The assistant dean decided not to tell her supervisor about this young man because he might feel embarrassed having to tell his fellow students why he was resigning in the middle of the academic year. She hoped his fall grades would soon lift him off academic probation.

Unfortunately, the young man received a D in Family Law and his grade point average fell even more after fall semester grades were in. The assistant dean knew this because he was one of the students whose grades she had checked herself, out of concern for him.

It was a big law school, and weeks could go by without her seeing any particular student.

But one morning a few weeks into the spring semester, she was walking across the law school atrium and saw this young man sitting by himself at his laptop computer. She crossed over to his table and got his attention. He took the iPod buds out of his ears, and she whispered, "You've got to get your grades up to a 2.0 this semester."

The student nodded, and she told him to please see her if he needed any help. She knew nobody else at the law school would make the same offer.

When she got back from her meeting, she found an e-mail from this student. The subject line was "Revealing Confidential Information in Public."

The student chastised her for doing just that, reminding her that under federal law, she could get into a lot of trouble – maybe even lose her job – for being as indiscreet as she had been with this student in the atrium.

At home that evening, the woman found her dog-eared old copy of *Jude the Obscure*.

The next morning, she resigned her position as assistant dean of students. She realized she could no longer in good conscience continue to set such a bad example for future attorneys.

Who Won't Kiss the Pig?

Jonathan, the 17-year-old boyfriend of Dayal Kaur's daughter Gurukirn, was the first one to notice the pig.

It was tied to the flagpole in the yard outside the gurdwara, the Sikh temple, not far from the picnic tables.

He'd had a good morning run and was just coming home – to the dismay of many members of the community, Dayal Kaur allowed Jonathan to live with her family once he and Gurukirn got pregnant – when he spotted the animal.

Too excited to bother with his usual stretching, Jonathan ran to their little house to tell his girlfriend's mother what he'd seen.

Dayal Kaur was swallowing her usual array of morning supplements – glucosamine and chondroitin for her arthritis, flaxseed oil for the omega-3 fatty acids for her heart, quercetin for her allergies, black cohosh for her hot flashes, lecithin for something that she had by now forgotten – when she heard, somewhere in the midst of Jonathan's breathless garbled braying, the word *pig*.

For a second she flashed on a demonstration against police brutality in Utica, New York sometime in the early Seventies. Then Dayal Kaur said: "A pig?"

Jonathan, still winded, nodded vigorously. "It's actually

cute." He was glad he could tell Dayal Kaur this without having to use her name.

Gurukirn was still asleep. She was in her seventh month and didn't wake up till noon.

As Dayal Kaur and Jonathan went down the block to the gurdwara to investigate, she realized what it meant.

"They think we're Muslims," Dayal Kaur said. "This is a hate crime."

"It's actually cute," the boy said again.

"We've got to report this," Dayal Kaur said, reaching for her cell phone. Jonathan was bending down to the animal with a look of delight on his face.

"Don't *kiss* it," Dayal Kaur told the father of her unborn grandson.

Albertson's Pulls Out
of New Orleans

I'll never forget June 11, 2002, the first day Desiree checked out my groceries. I'd missed the store's grand opening earlier in the day, but in the afternoon I was at the new Albertson's on Tulane Avenue near Jefferson Davis Parkway. I wanted to be reminded of home.

Pushing my shopping cart through the aisles, I felt transported back to Idaho, and I quickly snapped up my favorite store-brand foods, like the container of Dry Roasted Peanuts that beat the hell out of Planter's; the green plastic bags of Albertson's frozen veggies, including my favorite, Fiesta Mix; and the chocolatier-than-chocolate diet frozen yogurt.

If I thought I was in heaven then, well, you can imagine when I got into checkout line number 4 and discovered Desiree. Look, being a math major, I'm not so good at describing stuff, but to me, Desiree was a goddess, so beautiful that looking at her almost made me a little nauseous.

But it didn't stop me from noticing her big brown eyes, her lustrous hair, her breasts like a sparrow taking wing. She filled out her blue Albertson's polo shirt like it wanted to make love to her. Her name tag, DESIREE C., and below that the Albertson's motto, SERVICE FIRST!, told me almost everything I wanted to know.

As her hands guided my bags of frozen veggies over the

scanner, she managed to hit them right on the bar code every time. And after she rang up my collard greens and then my field peas with snaps, she looked up at me and smiled. For a minute I wondered if a geeky white boy from Boise would have a chance with her.

I'd gotten an Albertson's Preferred Card before I started shopping and had already put it on my keychain. When Desiree was finished, she took out a red pen and circled the amount I'd saved by being a Preferred Customer. She nodded and said, "Hope to see you again."

"Me too," I said. "Good luck."

It took me about four more visits to work up the nerve to tell her that my hometown was also the hometown of her employer, one of the biggest supermarket chains in the country. I explained how Joe Albertson had come to Boise during the Depression and opened his first store with $2,500 he borrowed from his wife's aunt. And how the old aunt's share was worth over a million dollars in company stock when she died.

Every week I'd park my Geo in the Albertson's parking lot. I knew that the people who want to keep New Orleans looking neat didn't like the idea of cars parking in front of the store because it didn't fit in with their idea of urban planning. And maybe they were right. People also complained that the store was dark, the prices high, the brand selection scant, the checkout lines intolerably long. But it didn't bother me one bit. It was Albertson's, after all, and my Desiree was worth the wait.

Besides, it wasn't always crowded. Once there was absolutely no one waiting for Desiree, and she obviously hadn't been busy for a while. She'd taken out Teen People from the magazine rack and when I got there, she was looking at a photo of Usher, naked from the waist up, his muscles gleaming.

It depressed me a little, but I started working out, doing a zillion stomach crunches to try to match Usher's abs. In the Albertson's pharmacy, when I picked up my Zoloft prescription, I also got some sunless tanning foam. I think Desiree noticed. One day she said, "You don't get Krispy Kreme anymore."

"No," I said, and I thought about lifting up my t-shirt, but I felt stupid doing it, especially because I wore briefs, not boxers like Usher, and I didn't wear my cargo pants low enough. The donuts weren't the first product I'd stopped buying because of Desiree – I switched maple syrups from Aunt Jemima to Log Cabin out of embarrassment – and her noticing their absence from my shopping cart made me determined to finally ask her out.

Our relationship had gone on a year already, after all, and we knew each other pretty well. She knew I liked Barilla elbow macaroni and that my favorite soda was the store brand Vanilla Max Cola, especially when they were on sale, three containers for two dollars. And I knew she liked chewing gum and had to wear a wrist guard for her carpal tunnel syndrome.

Desiree knew how loyal I was to Albertson's because I told her how creepy the crowds were at the Wal-Mart SuperCenter in the Lower Garden District and how the cashiers at the Winn-Dixie I went to before Albertson's opened used to be so lazy and inaccurate. I told her I wouldn't be caught dead at Langenstein's or Zuppardo's or the Whole Foods store where the help

~ 15 ~

all dressed weirdly.

And Desiree knew that no matter how long her line was – even if she had ten old ladies with tons of coupons in front of me – that I wouldn't get checked out by anyone else.

But things kept me from popping the question. Like I had a stomach virus that lasted like two weeks and she had to ring up my Sav-On Osco Anti-Diarrheal Capsules – Albertson's private label was just as good or better than Immodium, I knew – it sort of put a damper on romance, if you know what I mean.

When I started to feel better, I told myself as I drove down Tulane Avenue to the store, "This is the day you make the big move." But I had to go to the men's room before I finished my shopping, and that's when I noticed the sign outside it, near the room where the employees punched in and took their breaks.

TEAM ALBERTSON'S, it said, NOTHING YOU DO IN YOUR JOB IS WORTH GETTING HURT. Although under that it said PLEASE WORK SAFELY, I took it as a sign that moving our relationship to the next level might mean that either Desiree or I, or both of us, could really get hurt. So I figured I'd wait a little longer. Our minutes together were still special.

The next time I felt confident enough to ask her about getting together without the involvement of groceries, my face broke out in a kind of rash. I think the sunless tanning foam did more harm than good above my waist, although when I looked in the mirror, I could see the darker skin made my muscles look more defined. I tried to imagine Desiree's reaction when she saw me without a shirt for the first time. And I imagined her without her blue Albertson's polo shirt and drove myself wild.

The next time I saw her and handed her a roll of Brawny paper towels, I was about to tell her how much I wanted to see her outside the supermarket when the cashier in the next aisle called over to Desiree for help with a jammed register. Desiree hurried with the rest of my order and left me to the retarded bag boy. I was so rattled, I ended up with paper instead of plastic.

Finally one morning it got to be too much. This is it, I told myself as I scribbled my grocery list on a Post-It note, the way I always did. I'm going to tell Desiree how I feel about her and find out whether she feels the same way about me, I thought. I was pretty sure she did, but despite my new abs, I'm not the most confident sort of guy.

Still, I was ready to declare my love for Desiree, no matter what. I did some stomach crunches and then grabbed a bowl of Multi-Grain Cheerios ($3.19 with my Preferred Savings Card) and glanced at the morning paper.

I don't know what made me turn to the business section, because I never read it. But I glanced at its front page and saw a headline that made my head spin.

Albertson's was leaving New Orleans. It was selling its four stores in Gretna and the north shore to Sav-A-Center, but the three other stores would close. My store – my store and Desiree's – would be gone, just two years after it had opened with such promise.

An Albertson's executive said the company would only stay in markets where it could be the number one or two store. Here it was in fourth place with no hope of getting a large market share.

No hope? Were they kidding? There's always hope.

If Joe Albertson hadn't died in 1993, I'm sure things would be different. He would never make this the city that Albertson's forsook. Joe would have stayed and fought Wal-Mart and Winn Dixie and the rest.

Besides, who has to be number one or two immediately? You just need to get people to like you.

Everyone seemed really subdued when I got to Albertson's that afternoon. Oddly, Desiree didn't look unhappy. When I expressed my shock, she just shrugged and said, "Didn't you know? The store's been for sale for months."

I opened my mouth but nothing came out.

The next time I went in, I managed to ask Desiree what she was going to do in June when the store closed.

"Oh, I was moving to Vicksburg anyway," she told me as she scanned my three bottles of Albertson's drinking water. "My boyfriend's stepfather owns a lot of property there, and I'm tired of living here."

"Yeah," I said numbly. "Me too."

She had to call me as I was walking away because I forgot one of my bottles of drinking water. "Hey, you forgot something!" she said.

It occurred to me that she didn't call me by name, that she probably didn't even know my name although I'd sometimes paid with my Hibernia debit card with my name written right on it.

I'd lost Desiree. And maybe even worse, I'd lost Albertson's. Where would I get my special chocolaty frozen yogurt now? My Fiesta Blend frozen vegetables? My Zoloft?

Maybe, like Albertson's, I was a loser from Idaho who didn't belong here. I dropped off my groceries at home and then I walked and walked. Eventually, despite my depression, I realized I was hungry and so I went into the first restaurant I saw, some little Vietnamese place.

Because I'd been buying so many groceries to see Desiree, I hadn't eaten out in a really long time. The food at this restaurant was amazing: I had a Vietnamese po-boy made with grilled pork and a chunky, spreadable pate, all of it pressed between a crusty French roll with carrot strips, jalapeno, fresh cilantro and a cucumber cut like a pickle spear.

For dessert, the waitress recommended an icy strawberry mango shake. That's when I looked at her and fell in love. She told me her name right off: Thu. And I told her mine.

At the bottom of my shake was a pile of tapioca pearls that I slurped up greedily. Thu smiled as she brought me the check. I gave her the biggest tip I ever gave a waitress. "Come back soon," Thu said as I was about to leave the cash register.

Even though Albertson's and Desiree broke my heart, life goes on. I visit the Vietnamese restaurant a lot these days. I'm working up the courage to ask Thu out.

My Basic Problem

5 HOME

When I was a college freshman at a state university –
before I transferred to Barnard in my sophomore year –
I used to have all my classes after 2 p.m. every day. We
baby boomers were so numerous that the college had to
put us on two schedules, A and B. The A schedule was
mornings; B, afternoons. Freshman and lower
sophomores had to register in the B gym and take only
B – afternoon – classes. You stood on line in front of
tables set up by the various departments – Afro-
American Studies, Anthropology, Area Studies and so
on – and waited for hours, and finally you picked up
"course cards" that you could not fold, spindle or
mutilate. They were those IBM cards with a pattern of
rectangular holes that meant something to the
monstrous mainframe computers in the basement of
the gym. When you had all your course cards, you
would put them in a manila envelope with your
"registration card," which also had the little holes
punched out, and someone somewhere would match
you with the courses you were taking, provided nobody
had folded, spindled or mutilated the cards.

Since none of my classes were till 2 p.m. and I had the
hormones of a 17-year-old, I didn't wake up until 11
a.m.   I'd shower, eat a bowl of Froot Loops, do my
French homework (exercises of the *"Où est la bureau de
poste?"* variety) or write compositions in my dorm.
Then, at noon, I would turn on CBS and watch a soap

opera called *Where the Heart Is.*

Where the Heart Is was a new show back then, and it didn't last very long: I seem to be the only American who remembers watching it, so perhaps it existed only in my imagination. It was about Kate, a fragile blonde with whom I identified; her rotten boyfriend-stealing sister Alison; and their brother Julian, with whom they lived. Julian was chairman of the English Department on an ivy-covered campus, an expert on Byron, whose young wife, a concert pianist, was in love with his twentysomething son. Later Julian had an affair with the girl his son married. Julian also had an old alcoholic secretary who was in love with him.

My own freshman comp teacher was a Miss Stern whose name fit her demeanor; later, she went into publishing, editing celebrity biographies. She gave me a B. On my best essay, she wrote: "Beware of over-dramatization!"

They took *Where the Heart Is* off the air by the time I was a sophomore at Columbia, replacing it with *The Young and the Restless,* which I despised. But I was living with my boyfriend by then, so it hardly mattered that I could no longer watch Kate, Alison and Julian.

10 REM***THIS PROGRAM MEASURES NOTHING***

Or else I'm accused of being too lyrical. It's in me. What can I tell you? My mother died a few days after I was born.

I never had a mother to help me find the right blouse or skirt or pair of shoes in the morning, and my older sister only made my choices more difficult, so I was always late for everything. At the bottom of the stairs, my father -- who naturally was sort of like Julian on *Where the Heart Is* – would get impatient. "I'm coming!" I would always cry, and he would always yell back, "So's Christmas!" even though he'd been raised as an Orthodox Jew.

My very religious grandfather, when he felt I was telling a story too dramatically, would call me Thomashevsky. I thought this was a name Poppy Joe had made up, but last week or last month I read a *Miami Herald* article which mentioned Boris Thomashevsky, the leading actor of the Yiddish theater in America. He's been dead a long time now, like my grandfather and mother.

20 REM***VARIABLES: TOO MANY***

IF ABORTIONS ARE OUTLAWED, ONLY OUTLAWS WILL HAVE ABORTIONS was a bumper sticker I wanted to have made up. I dreamed it, literally.

In *Broca's Brain*, Carl Sagan wrote that it's impossible for a person to read words in her dreams. But I do, all the time. So I wrote to Carl Sagan, telling him to come investigate me, that I was perhaps the only one among billions and billions of living creatures who could read words in her dreams. Needless to say, he never replied.

I once went to an Oscar Awards party at the apartment of the daughter of America's most beloved TV weatherman. At the end of the evening she threw a tantrum because Sylvester Stallone didn't win Best Actor for *Rocky*. "*What* does Peter Finch need with a fucking Oscar?" she raged. "He's dead, dammit!"

Earlier in the evening she'd introduced me to the guy she used to live with by saying, "I'd like you to meet the father of my dead baby." Now she does the NFL pre-game shows while what's-her-name is on maternity leave.

I think of my interrupted pregnancies only when someone is using the phrase *biological clock*. Usually this phrase is used by people who believe every word of Carl Sagan's version of the universe.

I think of what my sister said on her last birthday before she disappeared: "Do you realize Martin Luther King was dead at my age?"

A month later Missy emptied her apartment of furniture and left this note for her nine-year-old daughter to find when she came back from Little League: *"Call your father and live with him for a while."*

30 INPUT "HOW MANY TIMES HAVE YOU GONE OVER THIS BEFORE?" ; X

For some reason, I still have a worn copy of the primer that I used to teach my niece how to read. I open it and see these sentences:

> *A rag is on a mat.*
> *Nat looks at the rag.*
> *Is it a rat?*

This stuff was supposed to teach kids how to read by using phonetics, or phonics. Except what sane boy would mistake a rag for a rat? But somehow Jennifer learned to read.

"I'm on the rag," I used to say to Lanny, who had never

heard the phrase before. He knew *curse, friend,* and the others, but didn't know from *rag.* In Great Neck, he had gone to high school with the father of the dead baby of the *Rocky*-loving lady sportscaster, a boy who – according to Lanny – went insane for two days every month.

I don't believe what men say about their girlfriends' periods. "If everything her boyfriend said about this woman were true," I told Lanny, "instead of covering the NFL for CBS, she would be on the Cable Health Network hosting *PMS Magazine.*"

Like my father and his father before him, Lanny never laughed at my jokes.

40 INPUT "WHO DID THIS TO YOU?" ; A$

Lanny's recent letters from New York read like those comprehension-testing passages on the Verbal section of the SAT or GRE. I always expect to find a multiple choice question after every paragraph:

The author of this letter recommends that you buy stock in:

A. Sunrise Savings and Loan, because of its real estate investments.

B. Carter-Wallace, because it makes Trojan condoms when everyone's scared of AIDS.

C. General Magic, because of its revolutionary proprietary software.

D. All of the above.

I read Lanny's letters out by the pool while I'm eating fruit. My favorite is kiwifruit, even though Lanny says they're now a cliché in Manhattan restaurant salads. They remind me of testicles, of course, so I take a knife

~ 24 ~

and slice them in half, then in quarters. The India-ink black seeds could be sperm cells waiting patiently for release from the green flesh. Kiwifruit have vitamin C and potassium, so unlike what's in men's testicles, they're good for you.

Starfruit is another favorite of mine. Most people make the mistake of peeling them. You don't need to. Just wash them off and slice horizontally. Lanny says that his latest girlfriend insists that starfruit are "merely decorative," but I think she is confusing them with herself.

Of course, summers in South Florida you can get an out-of-this-world mango. A good mango is unbearably good, but there's no more disgusting fruit than a bad mango. In that regard, mangoes are not unlike men.

50 POKE 33, 33

On my twenty-first birthday I had mononucleosis. They called it "kissing disease" back then, though I don't recall how I got it. At my birthday party I was about to blow out my candles when some really sweet and funny boy with long blond hair and granny glasses blew them out for me. "Public health reasons," he said, because of my mono. He was somebody's boyfriend or best friend, and I suspected he was gay.

Recently I wrote Lanny to ask if he knew what happened to that boy, and Larry said he was now – what else? – a corporate lawyer.

They were all so real before they became yuppies. Me, too.

Two months ago, Lanny had a two-hour layover at the airport in Miami, where I always feel like a foreigner. I went there to meet him. He was on his way to this extremely discreet bank in the Cayman Islands. Business, you know. He gave me one of those WHEN THE GOING GETS TOUGH, THE TOUGH GO SHOPPING T-shirts as a gift. I gave it to my niece.

Lanny justified voting for Reagan last year by saying he did it "for continuity's sake."

60 LET C = C + 1

I loved it when I got the flu on December 31. It saved me from driving to West Palm Beach for a New Year's Eve party. I slept for the first three days of the year.

In my condo I put up dark red, heavy curtains – think Scarlett O'Hara's ball gown – to block out the glare of the sun. Why are all Florida walls painted white? When I read the *Miami Herald* and touch the light switch or the door, it always leaves black fingerprints behind. *The New York Times Book Review* is even worse, although I'm probably getting what I deserve for reading it.

Sleeping at inappropriate times is my favorite thing. I am rumored to be in line for an appointment to the Nap Commission.

70 ? "THE PERSON YOU ARE, IS "; X + C - A$

And my Apple IIc, the little one, has 128K and all the right peripherals: dot-matrix Applewriter printer, joystick, Koala pad for drawing, even a modem I don't use. The monitor can't be beat.

Every day computers are making people easier to use. I love my little Apple IIc the way some women love their VCRs. My computer is an ironic machine, perfectly suited to me. I can take the little bugger to bed if I want and be assured that there are no bugs in the floppies I insert into it. I can take it with me in the car, on a plane, where the heart is. (The actor who played Julian is now a billionaire industrialist on another soap. His company makes electronic equipment.)

My Apple IIc responds to my every command, and when it doesn't, well, I'm the one who's at fault.

Lanny says I could make good relationships if I got on an electronic bulletin board: "It's better than bar-hopping because it's even more anonymous." You don't have to use your real name. If I ever log on, it will be as Julian Thomashevsky.

As the Cubans in Miami say, "Those that know, don't say. And those that say, don't know."

80 IF X + C - A$ = 0 THEN 30

I don't know, if you didn't know that already.

90 END

Many years later, as I faced my monthly condo board of directors meeting, I was to remember that distant afternoon when Lanny and I first made love.

It was in his parents' king-size bed in their bedroom in Great Neck. They were away in Aruba. The TV was on, but it wasn't playing *Where the Heart Is.* I smelled of strawberry body oil. We were high on grass and Boone's Farm Apple Wine. It started when he tickled my foot.

It's all an endless loop, no?

Roman Buildings

There

The sunlight was oppressive. I always wished it were nighttime. The streets were too white, too clean. I discovered that I had lost the keys to the condominium at The Moorings. How would my grandmother get back in? She was not Doris Lessing although they were both almost the same age. At one time or another they both said wise things.

My grandmother was at the acupuncturist's, downtown, by Lincoln Park. During the Convention the Zippies stayed there. On Mondays, my grandmother's acupuncturist would fly to Montgomery, to treat the crippled governor. Somehow their fates were linked, my grandmother's and the crippled governor's. Neither could walk.

A letter arrived from up North, from my school…my former school. It reminded me of my unfinished dissertation. The time limit was running out. If I did not do it that year, I would not get my degree. I felt a twinge of panic as I sat by the swimming pool. How did they know how to find me?

I could not finish my dissertation. I could not even imagine myself defending it, and I could not explain why. It was almost as if I would die if I completed the dissertation. I had forty pages of it written, but I hadn't written anything in over a year. There were numerous

Xeroxed chapters and articles in a manila envelope in
another state. I had not brought any of it with me to
Florida.

There was

One time Marie appeared to me as a character on a
soap opera Kathy and I were watching. Marie was
engaged to Skipper and was pregnant by him, although
I did not know if this was real or imagined. Perhaps
she was wearing a pillow underneath her dress. If it had
been real, I did not know if she was actually pregnant
by Skipper the person or merely by the character he was
portraying on the show. The dialogue between Marie
and Skipper did not reveal much. They were drinking
cocoa and talking about the problems of two other
characters, a man who accused another man of copying
him by bringing a whistle onto the dance floor of a
disco. The first man felt he was the only one in Ann
Arbor allowed to do that, and although he planned to
leave Ann Arbor, his friends were supposed to vote on
who would get the whistle next. It was going to be an
orderly succession, and the man who copied him ruined
that.

Marie was in my thoughts a lot then. She was my
former girlfriend's former husband's present lover. We
were an uncouple, Marie said, or rather, we once had
been. Or perhaps we were bookends, like the old
couple sitting together on the cover of that Simon and
Garfunkel album.

"It's your choice," Marie seemed to be telling me that
afternoon. I responded by telling her that was like a
choice between hedonism and Hasidism.

There was a

DeChirico courtyard. Twilight. Only it was a small
twilight, such as those on late autumn days in Rome. I
sat in something very much like a Roman building,
furnitureless, and thought about the draft in the Burger
King on Long Island where those boys in their flannel
shirts and patched-denim jeans had tormented me.
They were skinny boys like me, long-haired boys
without sideburns. They didn't know I had come there
only to use the bathroom after a night of sinus-clogged
sleep and piss hard-ons and struggles to stop dreaming
of Marie. They did not stop insulting me, these boys,
insulting me and insinuating themselves.

And yet there was a woman there – or a girl. I never
knew which to call her. She was like the person I had
sent letters to but never had seen, or had seen only once
and then at a time when she did not know me. We
made love there, but with our clothes on, the old dry
hump, the way Kathy and Donn did it when she was
sixteen and he was fifteen, before he left for Vietnam. I
could not come although I desperately wanted to. The
woman or the girl had several orgasms, growing more
exasperated with each one. Retarded ejaculation was a
more severe problem in those days than it generally is
today. Finally we gave up.

There was an herb

For once, I did not want a hamburger. I felt like an ice
cream soda. (If I had said this to Skipper, he would
have said, "Funny, you don't *look* like an ice cream
soda.") So I went into this luncheonette downtown,
the one on the ground floor of the old Florida Power

~ 31 ~

and Light building. I ordered a malted, not an ice cream soda.

The waiter, an old Cuban who was probably once rich, looked at me. "You can't order just a malted, *hijo*," he said. "There is a minimum here."

So I ordered a hamburger as well but I could not finish it. It was not that it tasted bad or that I was ill or that I was full. But at that specific point in time – as we used to say in the old days before there were recessions – I did not particularly want a hamburger. Back then I could complete nothing: eating a hamburger, writing my dissertation, making love. I was fixated on things in the past: feathered dinosaurs, the Late Archaic Indians, the Convention, and Marie, who was not really even a part of my own past but a part of the past of another person whom I barely knew.

What made it that way?

There was an herb store

In reality, one day I would pass Marie's parents' house, the one she lived in as a girl. It was raining very hard, for the first hurricane of the season had fortuitously hit the coast. There had been little property damage, however. I drove past the house and noticed Marie's father's car in the driveway, its rear lights on. I assumed that the headlights were on, too. I drove past the house again, and then I drove around the block another time after that, just to make sure I was seeing things correctly.

I went to a telephone near the causeway. The wind was blowing a splash of rain on my face. I dialed Marie's parents' number – which I knew by heart – and Marie's mother answered.

I said: *This is an acquaintance of Marie's you don't know me but I was passing your house just now and happened to notice that your car's lights were on I just thought you should know.*

Marie's mother chuckled and said she knew, that her husband was letting the car warm up because they had been having trouble with it. She thanked me anyway and asked my name. I did not give her my name but the name of the first patient of my second psychologist, a man who owned part of one of the then-newer hotels on Collins Avenue.

There was an herb store in

This is what I thought back then:

I thought that as an old man, I would one day look at a magazine with photographs of battered children on the cover, hurt-looking things with ugly welts, bruises, cuts on the forehead and cheek. Maybe they had broken bones. I would look at the beaten-up babies on the magazine cover and ask myself: *Is one of these my grandchild?*

But instead of that, I met Marie by the beach, the beach up in Hallandale where Skipper spent the night with someone I did not know. He did not tell me who it was or in what bar he found him, and I did not press the question. Marie pretended not to know me when she saw me by the beach up in Hallandale, and so I pretended not to know her, either. But I could see it wasn't her face, Marie's face, not her real face – as well as I could remember her, since we had only one brief meeting (I hesitate to say "encounter"), and that had been over two and a half years before.

I had a hard time getting to sleep that night, after I saw Marie by the beach up in Hallandale. I assumed that the insomnia was caused by my nausea, but the Pepto-Bismol did not help and neither did the coke syrup. The suppository might have worked, but by that time I realized it had been someone else, someone other than Marie.

There was an herb store in my

Marie, Marie – I held on so tight to her then, didn't I? Unable to let go, unable to be free of her, I did not know how to proceed. I kept hoping each time would be the last, the end, *fin*, the denouement, the conclusion.

One time Kathy showed me a photograph she had taken of us together, by the dig at the field preserve. Five layers had been uncovered, but the fourth interested me the most: the Late Archaic Indian civilization. We uncovered several artifacts, including some arrowheads, fragments of a bowl, and part of a human skull. Kathy could tell that the skull had belonged to a woman and that she had been killed by a blow to the head.

Marie's name was Elaine that day at the dig. But she had her own face. We were crouching together in Kathy's photograph. It reminded me of the Diane

~ 34 ~

Arbus photo of the twin girls. It also looked a little like one person with two heads.

We were both beautiful then and I was as attracted to Marie, or Elaine, as I was to myself. That day Kathy showed me the photograph I thought: *We could be one person, an androgynous amalgam of our separate selves.* I am embarrassed to say that I once actually thought things like that.

Immediately after seeing the photograph, I received a phone call. The caller hung up after I said hello. It was the second call like that that day. I had disregarded the previous one as a simple wrong number, but after the second call I was not so sure.

There was an herb store in my dreams

When I was young, Rilke admonished me nearly all the time. That *"You must change your life"* written so earnestly.

But mostly I was tired and preferred to close my eyes.

You must, Rilke would say.

But I just can't now, not right now, I thought.

You must change, he said.

Tomorrow. Tomorrow I'll do it.

Change your life, he kept saying.

Yes, yes. But not at this minute.

Your life, Rilke said.

So I reached for my pills, the little red triangular ones, the ones that helped me sleep. I swallowed two of them without water, and Rilke became silent.

There was an herb store in my dreams.

Always it was the same: endless rows of herbs in clear green-tinted glass jars, lining the walls, reaching to the ceiling. So many herbs, so many different colors and textures and tastes. I found myself in a kind of wonderland, for I wanted them all: to feel them against my body, to bathe in them, to drink teas prepared from them, to smell them, all of them.

The thousands of jars (perhaps more; I could not count them all) sat there, and they were mine: shepherd's purse, sorrel and sage; golden seal, sarsaparilla and sassafras; boneset, barberry bark, eyebright and fennel; sweet basil and quassia chips; chamomile and licorice and slippery-elm bark; elder flowers, dandelion root, ginseng and ginger; horehound and hawthorn; rose hips and rose petals and rosemary; papaya leaves, hyssop, anise, life-everlasting flowers…

I thought they were all for me, at least for a time.

Significant Others

There was a very long line at the bank, so Elspeth decided to go home and kill herself.

Elspeth worked the graveyard shift at the police precinct house. She had been having an affair with a married cop. "All cops are married," Elspeth always says. He told her that once his wife had the baby and they moved to the suburbs, he wouldn't be able to see Elspeth anymore. It was perhaps this that triggered the suicide attempt. Elspeth's trip to California for two weeks postponed her nervous breakdown for a couple of months, but the benign effects of the trip were already beginning to wear off when Elspeth walked into the bank, saw the long line, and decided to go back to her apartment and swallow the bottle of pills the doctor had given her for her migraines.

She swallowed the whole bottle, one pill at a time, and soon she became pretty groggy. Curiously, she felt better, less depressed. She called up Elihu to say goodbye to him. When she told him what she did, Elihu became oddly upset; it was strange to her why Elihu started yelling like that into her phone. She did not want to hear it, even though Elihu was her best friend.

Then some time passed and there was a knock at the door. It was Elihu and some policemen. She stood at the doorway, pale, blinking, looking at them look at her, and she told them all to go away, that she wanted to be alone.

The next thing Elspeth remembered was lying in a bed at Coney Island Hospital with her mother at her side. Her stomach had been pumped.

Elspeth started crying and her mother asked her what was wrong.

"Ma," she cried. "I want to move to a new apartment, not one so close to Elihu's."

*

I was giving my class their final, so I wanted to be there early. I drove up Flatbush Avenue in the snow, bought a cup of tea to take out, and was in my classroom at 8:45. Of course, no students were there. Except one. Billy DeMarco, the blond kid in the wheelchair, was sitting there in the dark before I got in. He hadn't been in class since October. I remember him telling me back then that he was driving to his father' s house in Pennsylvania and we discussed the roads in Jersey and I thought to myself that he must have hand controls on his car because otherwise how could he drive.

"I've been waiting twenty minutes for you," Billy said. "I've been really scared to face you."

I can't imagine anyone being scared to face *me*.

I looked at him. "You know I can't give you anything but a W after being absent all that time. It wouldn't be fair to the other students who showed up regularly."

"I guess I blew it," Billy said. His hands, folded in his lap, looked so pale. "It's my first term, and I thought it would be a snap, like high school, and I could get away with things. But I blew it."

I just nodded and helped wheel him out to the elevator.
When the elevator came, I wished him good luck.

*

Stanley looked much the same as ever when I saw him
at The West End. His complexion was pale and sallow,
but he kept off all the weight he lost on the Weight
Watchers diet. Yet somehow there seemed to be an
invisible layer of fat surrounding his body. He still
carried that green bookbag, although that one must
have been the sixth or seventh bookbag he's had.

Stanley should have graduated in 1971, but there were
so many F's and Incompletes on his transcript, I figured
he'd probably never graduate. Every term he took just
one course or another leave of absence. At that time
only going to films every day sustained him. His friend
worked for the Catholic Film Office, formerly the
Legion of Decency, and so he got into all their
screenings for free. Stanley said the priests and nuns
especially loved when the films made jokes about the
Pope.

We always said that Stanley is the one person who
never changes. But Stanley confided that he was doing
something to change his status. He was finally in
therapy – "to make sense of incoherence," Stanley told
me.

"You should have been in therapy five years ago," I
said.

Stanley took a sip of beer and admitted that he was
been on the verge of a nervous breakdown for years
and had only been functioning marginally. Six months
before, he started to have phobias about going places,

and that's when he decided to see this male psychiatrist in Manhattan.

During their first session, when he told the psychiatrist of his obsession with films, the doctor asked, "Didn't you used to write movie reviews for The Columbia Spectator?"

"That endeared the man to me forever," Stanley told me. "And besides, being in therapy gives me something to talk about other than films."

*

On Tuesday night Ken's dog's ear started bleeding, so they rushed it to the vet, who said the dog had a tumor.

On Thursday, Ken's mother was about to make the decision to put the dog to sleep when Ken burst into the vet's office and said he didn't want that to happen. The doctor said that he didn't know if a dog Rascal's age could survive an operation to remove the tumor. Despite the dog's heart condition and frailty, Ken insisted on the surgery. The dog was operated on, and Ken took her home to convalesce.

On Monday, the vet said the biopsy proved negative: the tumor was benign. Ken's mother said he looked pale when he got off the phone with the vet, and that night Ken came down with another of his colds.

On Friday, Ken told me he was feeling better but was having a terrible time with his mother, whom he said had become "a real sickie." She was so annoyed with the dog keeping her up nights that she wanted to put Rascal to sleep. Ken of course yelled at her and then she tried to induce guilt by crying or calling up Ken's aunts and telling them how rotten Ken treated her. That morning, when Ken left for grad school, his mother said, "Say goodbye to the dog because I'm calling the SPCA and she won't be home when you return." When Ken rushed home after his last class, the dog was still there.

On Sunday, the tumor on the dog's ear grew back. It was malignant after all.

The next day Ken's mother had the dog put to sleep. Ken carried on terribly.

Two weeks later Ken called me to say that he couldn't function very well, that he felt depressed and guilty over the dog's death, that he missed Rascal, that he felt such hostility toward his mother. He had decided to see the same psychiatrist he saw when he was breaking up with Aurora and hyperventilating. Ken said he was almost ashamed to confess this to me, but he had begun to look up into the sky and talk to the dog during the day.

Exactly one week and one day later, Ken called me again with what he said was "very good news." He and Sylvia had gotten engaged and would be married around Christmastime in a small ceremony in a rabbi's study. He didn't say a word about the dog.

*

I used to like sitting at the counters of Greek diners.

Coming out of the Thalia after an afternoon double bill – Stanley was not there – I went across the street to a diner and sat down at the counter next to this pasty-faced middle-aged guy who wouldn't stop talking.

A typical New York nutjob, he had a grudge against the very rich, knew how to solve the problems of the Middle East, and had traveled the world "from Casablanca to China, seeing everything in between." I just kept nodding as he went on and on, usually beginning his sentences with a "Whattayathink…," as if I'd just contradicted him.

Finally he told me he had been captured in the Battle of the Bulge. He was taken to a Nazi POW camp, where he was tortured by a sadistic commandant: "Whattayathink, it was *Hogan's Heroes*? An Australian RAF pilot couldn't take it anymore and committed suicide by flinging himself on a live electric wire."

I figured that witnessing that must have unhinged this man's mind. He needed psychiatric help.

The man made me think of the Ancient Mariner. When I left the diner, he was telling a woman who had just walked in everything he had told me. What was the point of telling the same story over and over?

*

I had to meet Professor Wolfson for our tutorial at 3 p.m., and I was running a bit late. When I got to his office, he told me my novel was unpublishable because of the too-generous "slice-of-life" material and the many characters. He thought it was a very personal book, and felt that the parts about Shelli, Ronna, Avis and Helene were the best – though I constantly undercut myself by giving other people's problems and intrigues equal weight to the protagonist's.

He also said I try to write too much like real life, going back to characters the reader doesn't remember from the first brief mention.

I told him, honestly, that I wasn't discouraged, that I was certain I'd have a publishable novel in another incarnation of the material, and besides, I joked, I had great LSAT scores and could always go to law school if writing fiction didn't pan out.

After leaving Professor Wolfson's office, I went down to Boylan cafeteria for a drink and was joined by Elayne. We were talking when the 4 p.m. news came over the college radio station. I heard the story about "the suicide…nineteen-year-old boy…Walter Dreyfus…had gone to counseling but there was no help available…parents said he'd been depressed…killed instantly."

Elayne later said that I got so pale she thought I was going to faint. A delayed reaction hit me – Walter Dreyfus – *Wally! Jared's brother!*

I felt sick to my stomach.

Not knowing where else to go, I wandered back to Professor Wolfson's office and told him what had happened. "Incredible!" he said. "One of the characters in your novel!" He let me use his phone.

I called Ken and his mother was crying. "I hope you're not going to tell me what Elihu did," she was saying. "This will be a terrible blow to Ken."

I called Stanley and he said that he'd read the story in *The Daily News* this morning and made the connection immediately. Stanley said he wouldn't go to funerals, that he never goes to funerals, hates seeing those scarily pale dead bodies in their caskets. "But I think *The Loved One* is a great film," he told me.

I called Elspeth and she said, "Why do people do such stupid things?" I reminded her about the migraine pills she swallowed. "That was different," she said. "It was quiet. It wasn't like jumping off the roof of the Student Center."

Professor Wolfson was writing things down on a yellow pad as I talked – probably notes for a lecture to his undergrad lit class.

There were other calls to make, but I had to go home and mark my own class's finals. I read their papers over and over again before I gave most of them A's. I kept repeating to myself, out loud: "Shit…shit…shit…"

What was Wally thinking of?

The Life of Katz

He is born and grows up. He marries Catherine, his
childhood sweetheart. They live in Greenwich Village
as he doggedly pursues an acting career. He gets a bit
part as the doctor in a production of *Cat on a Hot Tin
Roof.* His next role, Dogberry in *As You Like It*,
catapults him into theatrical stardom. He and Catherine
regularly put on the dog and dine on expensive steaks at
The Cattleman. On spring afternoons they walk all
over New York until their dogs hurt and they have to
take catnaps under dogwood trees in Central Park.

They have a baby, a son, and move to Brooklyn.
Catherine insists the boy get a Catholic education, but
Katz cannot abide dogma and hates Father Malley, that
hypocrite in the dog collar; still, Junior has his first
catechism. Father Malley likes to hit the boy with his
cat-o'-nine-tails. Junior becomes a strange, withdrawn
child. He is forever going around their new house with
hangdog looks; he spends hours in the backyard,
dissecting caterpillars.

Katz tries to be a father to his son for his wife's sake.
He takes the boy to Yankee Stadium to watch Catfish
Hunter pitch but gets angry when Junior puts catsup on
his hot dog. Junior says he would rather be home
writing some doggerel or in the library, bending over
the card catalog or reaching for some dog-eared book.
"Doggone it," Katz tells his wife, "there's no reasoning
with that kid."

Meanwhile, his own career moves in a new direction: playwriting. The results are disappointing; after five years, he has two dogs and one turkey to his credit. The audience subjects him to catcalls. His life goes to the dogs. He can't even get small parts as an actor anymore. Catherine is unsympathetic. "It's a dog-eat-dog world," she tells him.

He takes up with a chorus girl, a cheap floozy who plays cat-and-mouse with him for a while. One dog day afternoon, they come out of a motel together, and Junior, walking home from school, spots them. The father categorically denies everything, but his son does not believe him. Finally Katz admits the truth and tells Junior to let sleeping dogs lie.

But Junior lets the cat out of the bag, and Katz is in the doghouse with Catherine. She leaves him, taking Junior to Catalonia, where a catastrophe occurs: on a catamaran on the Mediterranean, on their way to the Catacombs, there is a terrible accident. They both drown. Neither knew so much as the dog paddle.

Katz breaks down at the funeral when he sees the two coffins on the catafalque. He is taken to a mental hospital. For eight months he is catatonic. Then who should come to visit but Father Malley, whom he hadn't seen in a dog's age. The priest has mellowed with time and helps him get over the cataclysmic events of his life. Katz grows old. He is sent to a nursing home in the Catskills. He develops cataracts. He becomes senile. Dying, his last words are: "It's a dog's life."

Father Malley presides at the funeral. "*Odi et amo*," he says in his eulogy, quoting Catullus. "That's life," a mourner says as the coffin is put into the ground next to the other two graves. "Whether you're an underdog or sitting in the catbird seat, you end up in the same place." "*Requiescat*," Father Malley says.

Those Seventies Stories

JOHN

John and I both lived alone. Each of us ate dinner at the counters of neighborhood diners. All of the diners in our neighborhood were owned by Greeks and all of them looked the same: the Arch, the Venus, the Five Brothers, the Californian, the Athena, the Ram's Horn.

When I went to diners, sometimes I wore my glasses and sometimes I wore my contact lenses. I convinced John, who was an actual idiot, that I was two separate people, identical twin brothers who hated one another.

When John would say to me, "I saw your brother at the Athena last night," I would say, "Aah, don't talk to me about that creep."

Then John would say: "Brothers was meant to be friends. I woulda been friends with my brother but he died when we was just kids. Got run over by a tractor, y'know?"

I knew, I knew: John had told me the story at least twenty times before.

One time Vivian, the fat waitress at the Arch, said, "I talk to my dog all the time."

"Yeah, me too," John said. "But the difference is my dog talks back to me!" Then he asked her: "So, Vivian, are you getting rich?"

Vivian snorted and said something like, "This snow is killing us. Monday no business, Tuesday no business, Wednesday no business... If it snows again, I'm gonna kill myself."

"Nah, don't do that," John said. "But just in case, can I have your apartment?"

"My apartment," Vivian said, spitting out the two words. "My apartment is even worse than yours."

John turned to me and I knew one of his moronic questions would follow. "Tell me," he said, "can you tell me who the guy is who puts flowers, roses, on Marilyn Monroe's grave every day?"

I nodded. "Joe DiMaggio."

"What about the other one?"

"What other one?" I asked.

"Me," John said, pointing to his grizzled face. He had hardly any teeth.

Another time John asked Myrtle, the redheaded waitress at the Ram's Horn if her daughter was working now.

"My daughter?" Myrtle replied. "She can't work."

"Why not?"

"She's lazy. Lazy people don't work. She sits around on her ass all day."

"Why don't ya do something about it?" John asked Myrtle. "Why don't ya use your hand?"

"My hand? Better I'll use my luggage and tell her to get out. Eighteen and she don't want to work. Ever hear anything like it? Well, she's not gonna get another dime from me."

John sipped his cold coffee – he liked it cold – and then said, "But ya didn't say you wouldn't give her any quarters and nickels." After which he elbowed me in the ribs, nearly upsetting my bowl of New England clam chowder.

I laughed falsely, but John didn't know the difference. He appreciated an audience. "See, your brother's a sourpuss. He don't have a good sense of humor like you do."

"My brother's a cocksucker," I told John and went back to my clam chowder.

One night at the Five Brothers, John asked the waitress, Reba, if her son still wanted to be a priest.

"Yeah," Reba said, serving me my cheeseburger de luxe and drawing me a large Tab. "I told him if he keeps it up I'm gonna take him to a psychi—a psychi—a psychologist."

"Priestes can have fun," John assured her. "Years ago I used to see all these priestes at the burlesque."

"They're not *priestes*," I said. "They're fucking *priests*, you moron. One syllable."

John wiped his nose with the back of his hand. Motioning towards me, he said to Reba, "Wouldya believe this guy's got a brother who's real nice? No wonder the two of 'em can't get along."

"We fight like catses and dogses," I said sarcastically.

John ignored me and went on with Reba. She wore too much makeup and her skirts were too short. "Reba," he said, "maybe your son wants to be a priest so he can marry you off again."

"I don't want to get married no more.'

"Aah, come off it, Reba, you girls gotta fall three or four times."

"I already had my three or four times."

John coughed a sick man's cough. He was always unshaven. Appearing to think for a moment, he said, "You girls can't live without us men. Why, if it wasn't for you girls, we men could go around without any trousers. It's because of you we have to wear 'em. Otherwise we could just go around naked."

Reba laughed. I swallowed some French fries and said, "Oh, so *that's* why we wear trousers!" I was being deliberately nasty. "Jeez, I'd always wondered! It's such an education, sitting here with you, John! Why don't you say something else stupid?"

John just shook his ugly old head. "If you was your brother you wouldn't talk to me like that. Your brother's a real gentleman."

"My brother's a cocksucker," I said as I pushed my glasses up the bridge of my nose.

John just sat there after that, ready to spit.

The next night, at the Venus, he complained about how my brother had mistreated him the day before.

TONYA

Tonya's real name was Maria but she hated Maria. "Every other Puerto Rican girl is named Maria," she told me. "Besides, I *feel* like a Tonya." This was before Patty Hearst.

When Tonya was about sixteen years old she became pregnant from a fellow who she said knew less about life than she did: "All we knew was that kissing felt good and it brought out other ideas about sex."

Pregnant, Tonya felt the world was coming to an end. Everyone was against her: the boy's mother, his sisters, his entire family. They insisted that Tonya had seduced him, that she talked him into having sex. The boy was two years younger than Tonya.

Tonya's family went on a warpath of their own. Her mother continued to rant and rave about how she would refuse to let the boy "get away with it." Both families wanted revenge: they took out warrants and there was a knife fight between Tonya's uncle and the boy's brother. Tonya's mother told the judge it was statutory rape. The boy's mother said he was involuntarily seduced. "It was just an experiment," Tonya cried to the judge, but both the mothers were going berserk and couldn't hear her.

Tonya's mother wanted them to get married. The boy's mother wanted Tonya in a home. Tonya resolved to herself that neither one of the mothers would get what she wanted. She just kept repeating to herself, "Everything must come to an end. Everything must come to an end." Eventually, she thought, if she repeated the phrase enough times, it would have to come true.

Tonya's baby took its father's last name. He said he would support the baby after he graduated from school and got a job. The baby was a victim of circumstances, Tonya said. That was where I came in.

"What do you know about raising a baby?" I said to Tonya the first day she showed up at my desk in the social services office.

"What do *you*?" she spit out. I liked them when they acted up like that. I thought I heard her mutter "faggot" under her breath.

"Why aren't you living with your mother?" I asked her. I was making sure to frown.

"I can't relate to my mother," Tonya told me. "She thinks I'm the only one in the whole world ever to get pregnant without having a wedding. She keeps carrying on like a crazy lady."

Tonya's heavy perfume was the only thing I could smell that day. I stared at her faint mustache and shook my head. Then I tapped the pencil on my desk. It was *my* desk, after all.

Tonya continued: "She wants me to drop out of school, man. My life ain't an extension to her future. She's got this terrible hangup, she cries and prays for me all the time. The Roman Catholic Church is supposed to solve everything. To her, I committed a sin and she talks all day to God and the Virgin Mary to forgive me…"

"Yeah?" I said, nodding. "Go on."

But Tonya wouldn't cry; she knew I was hoping for that. Instead, her voice just got louder. "Her attitude is really negative, y'know? I mean, I want some kind of career in the future – what, you think that's so funny?"

"Was I smiling?" I asked innocently. "I didn't realize."

"She's just like you, you cocksucker, putting all these obstacles in my path. She won't babysit, she wants me to go to work…Oh, fuck it, man, I'm not telling you any more of this!" Then she ran out.

I knew she'd be back, of course. It was a couple of months later. She looked more than a couple of months older. She wasn't wearing perfume and her mustache had gotten just a shade darker.

"So I'm working in this lousy factory from four o'clock to twelve o'clock midnight. It's in this basement and all the other workers are men, nine of them. We make booster cables. During the day I go to school. And it's hard, but I'm going to get my freaking diploma and I'm going to go to college…"

"Really?" I said. "I'm sure the Ivy League universities must be all excited over *that* possibility. And the child?"

"Johanna? She's just great, she's not like you or my mother. Johanna's my means of having someone to talk to. I release my emotions with her mainly, my ideas for the future... You see, my Johanna don't laugh at me."

I smirked. "Babies her age aren't *able* to laugh. If she could, she probably would."

"You bastard."

I thought she was going to spit at me and I got excited, but she wasn't quite up to it. Too bad. Instead, she went on talking: "See, Johanna just looks at me and she helps me more than you do. She understands my suffering. She is gonna know the real truth about this, about me being unfairly punished..."

This time it was me who left the desk. It was my lunch hour and I didn't want to miss seeing John at the Arch. When I came back from lunch – without my glasses, I was the nice brother that day – my desk was as tidy as ever. She hadn't touched a thing.

Tonya got transferred to another caseworker, a black woman who was supposedly very sympathetic. This woman later told me that Tonya was keeping a notebook in which she recorded all of her frustrations. Tonya titled the notebook *The Imprisonment of My Mind*. When Tonya read back what she had written so angrily, my colleague explained, she could understand herself better. She was beginning to deal with her mother.

Yeah yeah, I thought. But what I said was: "I always liked Tonya, but I got the feeling she could never quite open up with me. Probably because I'm a man." The black woman agreed.

The last time I saw her, Tonya came over to my desk while she was waiting for her caseworker to get finished with another client. "I'm going to college," she announced defiantly.

I just shrugged. "You call your own shots."

"Oppressor!" she yelled. The whole office turned around to look.

Three years after that, she ran for the city council as a Communist. I didn't live in her district, but I wrote her in anyway.

COUSIN ALAN

My first cousin once removed Alan was a few years older than me. Unlike myself, he was crazy.

Uncle Fred made Alan crazy, him and Aunt Mary. Uncle Fred was also paranoid but somehow he managed to function for most of his life. He and Aunt Mary were retired by the 1970s. They would go to sleep at 7 p.m., awaken at 3 a.m., have lunch by 10 a.m. and eat supper in mid-afternoon. That was a sure sign of insanity.

As a kid, Alan could never play with anyone else because Uncle Fred and Aunt Mary wouldn't let him get dirty with other kids' germs. Aunt Mary followed him around with a washrag soaked in Lysol. Alan wore rubbers when there was one cloud in the sky and he had to have a sweater on always, even when it was ninety degrees out.

When the teacher at our school – Alan was two grades ahead of me – told Uncle Fred that Alan needed a psychiatrist, Uncle Fred hit the ceiling. "My son isn't crazy!" he shouted. *"Psychiatrists* are who's crazy!" He tore up the rollbooks on the teacher's desk.

One summer Alan actually went to the same sleepaway camp that I did. On Visitors' Day the camp director told my mother: "If I had Alan away from those parents for just one year, I could make something of him. As it is, he'll end up in a loony bin." Of course my mother couldn't say a word about it to Uncle Fred.

Naturally, Alan did end up in a psychiatric institution, spending most of his adolescence there. *Paranoid/schizophrenic* was the diagnosis. He was let out, for some odd reason, when he turned twenty-five. I never got to go to the place because my mother said I shouldn't see what went on there. I would have liked to.

Alan ended up saying he was a minister in some obscure Christian cult. He closed all his letters to his parents – they refused to see him – with drawings of stars and comets and crosses and the message, "Jesus can save even your lives." Prior to this he had been a Buddhist.

There were tattoos up and down Alan's skinny arms. He had the words HATE and LOVE on his knuckles, HATE on his right hand, LOVE on his left, like in the old Robert Mitchum movie.

Uncle Fred refused to deal with Alan, and because of my work, Uncle Fred assigned me the task of giving Alan his money.

But I would not go to Alan's apartment, of course. He shared it with two prostitutes who sometimes beat him up. Alan would come to my office. Everyone assumed her was a client and not a cousin. He was actually a client in a different office.

I treated Alan like any other client except that he got cash from me.

Alan carried a cane with a sword inside it. Why? "To protect me from mine enemies," Alan told me. If a man brushed him by on a crowded sidewalk, Alan would start a fistfight that he'd almost always lose. For a while all he talked about with me was UFO's.

"Don't you think there are people on other planets?" Alan asked me. "People who are better than these fuckers here on earth?"

"Maybe," I said.

Alan frowned. "Come on, there's *gotta* be. It can't just be earth, earth, like that's all there is. Jesus foretold the coming of UFO's. It's right there in black and white in your Bible."

I responded by handing Alan the envelope with the money in it. "Your parents want you to spend this carefully, now. Not like last time. No more blowing it all in one night."

"Jeez," Alan said, his eyes wild as usual but with tears in them for a change. Although Alan was older than I am, he thought I was the older one. I sat at a desk. I was an authority figure. Alan listened to me. Both of us were only children.

Every time Alan would leave the social services office, he shook my hand with a different unusual grip. He told me he knew fifty different grips and that if I wanted, he could teach me all of them.

"I don't get much call for shaking hands," I told my crazy cousin.

At Sunday dinner at my mother's house, my mother would always say, "It's a pity on poor Alan." Then she'd look at me and say, "Sometimes you've just got to be grateful."

The food at my mother's was better than at the diners, but the company was nowhere as interesting.

MYSELF

Back then I was a solid citizen. I even voted in school board elections. Before anyone else did, I ate only whole wheat bread. I jerked off twice a day, just before bed and then again when I first woke up. I didn't want to get into any kind of trouble.

I wore corduroy sports jackets and ties that were neither too narrow nor too wide. I had a master's degree in social work. I went to high school reunions, got regular haircuts, read the newspaper every single day. At night, I read good classic literature, not crap, really good writers like Carlyle. He was impotent, you know.

To enlarge the fraction of your life, Carlyle said, don't try to increase the numerator. Instead, decrease the denominator. I attempted to do that every day back then.

At night I would dream that I was making love to my twin brother. Sometimes, though, my brother looked like Alan and not me. All I knew in those days was that I loved this dream-brother totally, the way a man should love his actual brother.

When my phone rang one day at work, it was Tonya. "I'm now in medical school in Riverside, California," she told me. "But I wanted to phone you to let you know there's still a chance I could love you."

"I'm busy right now," I said, even though it was my lunch hour. "Call back later."

A few minutes after that, I was walking in the street and John passed me by. He had no face. "I know you," John said to me.

"You must be mistaken," I told him.

"No, I *know* you," John insisted. "You look exactly like your brother."

That was the day my life ended, or maybe the day it actually began.

A Wake in One Zone

SLEEPYHEAD—I WENT OUT FOR A WALK
WITH YOUR GRANDFATHER, the note on the
hotel room dresser said. She smiled dreamily and
remembered something pleasant. The traveler's alarm
clock, that small green triangle, said it was 3:40. She
had gone to sleep with a headache after lunch; Robert
had been doing needlepoint on the other bed. The
hotel room had two beds, one single and one double.
Now Robert was gone.

She saw him naked the first time the night before, as
she was about to begin her nightly entry in her diary:
February 13, 1974. He was changing out of his briefs
into another pair. All boys wore the same white briefs
with the same red-and-black stripe on the waistband
that looked purple from far away. Johnny wore them,
and so did Chris, and so did her little brother. The light
was so low the night before, only the weak amber of the
dresser lamp. Without her glasses it wasn't all that
clear. But Robert had looked so beautiful, so
vulnerable, naked like that, it had almost made her cry.

She was still a virgin. Johnny and she had been only
kids, and he got impatient but tolerated it. At least he
had until he left her for Sally. ("Why do you like Sally?"
she asked him later, foolishly. "I don't really know,"
Johnny said, "but I guess mostly because she can be a
bitch." Implying that she was not, and that she could
never be.) So she and Johnny made do, and they both

managed their not insignificant satisfactions. There were fine moments with Johnny.

Chris was a virgin, too, and never touched her. She was about to tell him how she wanted him to pounce on her sometimes, but gently. Soon she met Robert, and Chris was in the past.

Robert went further, and tried other things, for he had had experience. But he never persisted against her resistance, the hand gently taken off the place where she did not want it to be. Even the night before, when they shared the double bed, he did not do anything she did not want him to do. And what they did was good.

When Johnny said goodbye for good, he told her she was an anachronism. That hurt. But she had been reading *Jude the Obscure* at the time, and she liked Sue Bridehead, and so it did not hurt all that much. She and Robert almost broke up over it twice, but each time he said he still wanted to be with her even if she wouldn't. The Sisters had been right about that, and Robert wasn't even a Catholic boy. Lately Robert had been trying to appeal to her sense of logic, telling her how ridiculous it was to do everything else and not that and still call yourself a virgin. She didn't argue with him. She couldn't. But she knew what she felt—it wasn't conscience, it wasn't morality, it wasn't fear of commitment or pain. It had to do with her being she, a sense of herself and what she was and the things she knew she could not do. But mostly it had to do with her world being all pastel: lilac and lemon yellow and wispy essence of smoke.

Robert's world was white mice in mazes, and unfinished meals with half-eaten platters, and those serrated edges where the logical met the absurd. Their worlds were only coterminous at a few points, but those were enough for both of them—at least they had been so far. Johnny's world had been black light and blue smoke and plucky seagulls taken flight in a storm. But then his world changed, and she did not belong. Chris' world she remembered only vaguely: it was knee socks and sassafras tea and lived-in upholstery.

Was it all because she was still not awake? Was it stage one or stage four that she was in? She would have to get Robert to explain it again, and he would grow impatient, but then be glad that she cared. It seemed like stage one to her: the mental drifting, the shallow breathing, the occasional jerk upwards.

SLEEPYHEAD—I WENT OUT FOR A WALK WITH MY GRANDFATHER. Yes, that was it. *Robert's* grandfather. Both of her grandfathers were dead, both before she was born. Robert still had two grandfathers, one short and one tall. She wondered which grandfather it was. She murmured something. But she had a grandmother, and Robert did not.

She thought of herself as three people, and a moment passed, the traveler's clock ticking, and she thought: What a strange and pleasant idea. And she closed her eyes again. Her glasses were on the dresser and she was glad to be free of them. They were causing red indentations on either side of her nose, indentations which did not fit in with her freckles.

She opened her eyes, focused on Robert's navy blue sweater, the crew-neck lying on the floor by the bed. She stared at the blue, closed her eyes, opened them to the ceiling, and saw a patch of orange. The opposite of blue. As Robert was Johnny's opposite, as she was Sally's, as God was—whose?

~ 63 ~

More sleep, she felt. It was necessary after the night before, and the headache was there still, a bit, not yet gone. But still she fought it. She looked at the note again.

SLEEPYHEAD—I'VE GONE OUT FOR A WALK WITH MY GRANDFATHER. It was in the perfect tense now. She had not noticed it before. Of course Robert would write in the perfect tense, just as Johnny would have used the pluperfect, just as Chris would have used... She didn't know any more what tense Chris would have used. Probably, she thought, the simple present: I WALK WITH MY GRANDFATHER. But Chris had no grandparents— the Germans saw to that.

"Cleft in twain." That was the phrase that stuck stone in her head. Could one be cleft in *train*? In transit? Sic gloria transit? "Oh, sic, sic, sic," she mumbled, admonishing herself for the play. Her hand, under the pillow, was asleep, all darning needles and rolling pins. The hand was still red and swollen, and not a part of her anymore. And though it frightened her to be like that, she didn't budge. A move was more than she could make. Always, it seemed.

She thought of New Jersey. They came up to the hotel through No Jersey. No, *New* Jersey. Robert and she had stopped at a Howard Johnson's, and they had licked their frozen baked-beans-on-a-stick, and the hostess with the orange-and-blue face smiled at them, but severely, as if to admonish with guilt. How she wished she could be a bitch! But she did not have the things that Sally had, and she could not afford to be anything but nice. At the moment she was nice and tired. Good and tired. Extraordinarily tired. Horribly tired, fantastically tired, terrifically tried. But she was not sick and tired. At least she was too young for that.

This time, when she looked, it said: SLEEPYHEAD— I'VE GONE OUT FOR A TALK WITH HER GRANDFATHER. She squinted. There was a pain somewhere. So that was it. Outside the window it was snowing, thick globs of white which looked so heavy, so massive. Robert had gone out to speak with someone else's grandfather. Probably in the lobby or the snack bar, or maybe in the sauna. But "a talk"— that meant it was something more than casual. Apparently a discussion of some significance. The thought entered, and then she knew, and silently she cursed herself for not thinking of it long before.

Sally's grandfather. Yes, that was it. The violinist, that old man with the thick white eyebrows. Robert was going to see Sally's grandfather to ask for Sally's hand. She chuckled involuntarily at the joke, but then, cranky, she began to cry. She cried like a colicky infant. Robert was leaving her for Sally, just as Johnny had done the year before. The same thing was happening all over again. An aria da capo. An old wound, long thought to have been healed, burst open anew. Blood everywhere, and she had forgotten to buy her tampons. She moaned with the ache from the growing pains. The pain was bad. Like a prayer, she repeated the name of the state, first New Jersey, then Jersey alone: Jersey, Jersey, Jersey, Jersey, Jersey, Jersey, Jersey, Jersey...until the word sounded foolish and foreign and absurd, and she felt feverish and obsessed and in hell.

But she reached for her glasses, and she looked at the note: SLEEPYHEAD—I WENT OUT FOR A WALK WITH YOUR GRANDFATHER. She had been right the first time. Robert would be back.

She turned over the pillow. The headache was gone.
She could smile.

Life with Libby

October 1971

I meet Libby. My friend Jared introduces us at a
winemaking class at the Student Center. I like Libby. All
through the winemaking class we sit on the floor. I
watch Libby. From time to time she rests her arm on
Jared's. Then she leans against him, holds his hand.
Jared is intently studying the winemaker's words, as if
he's memorizing them. I am looking at him with Libby.

She is making him happy, I think. I like the way she
looks. She is my height, a little blonder than I am, with
two long braids tightly wound; she is just about right or
maybe ten pounds overweight; her legs are long and
well-muscled; there are wispy blond hairs on her legs.
Libby wears granny glasses, round but small. There are
laugh lines around her eyes that you can see when she
takes her glasses off to wipe the lenses on Jared's
flannel shirt. Her mouth is small; above her lip, in the
place where the indentations are, the part of the face
that I used to think had no name but which I've since
learned has an ugly name I can never remember, is a
mole that protrudes from the skin. Usually I don't like
moles, but Libby's is sweet.

She is wearing one of the granny dresses I become used
to seeing all that fall, when she is always at Jared's side. I
am happy for Jared but envious. Myself, I am going

through a bad time. I am nineteen years old and will probably never love again.

May 1972

It seems as if Jared has always had Libby. Libby and I rarely talk because there is nothing for us to talk about. She is an art education major. I am a political science major. We have a lot of the same friends now, so we see each other nearly every day on campus and often at weekend parties. Libby likes me but then she likes everybody.

She touches me a lot when we talk. Because I don't get touched often, I love her for that and find myself taking pleasure in Libby's casual hugs. Jared does not mind Libby hugging me or anyone except Leonard. Leonard is going with Vicky anyway so Jared does not have to worry.

One afternoon at an almost-the-end-of-the-term party, Libby can't find a seat and so she sits on my lap. She notices that a button near my belly has opened and says, "That's cute." I am embarrassed and close my shirt. Jared laughs. Libby and I share a lime that is left at the bottom of an already-drunk lime rickey. It tastes sweeter than a lime should taste. I put it in my mouth. Libby puts it in hers. I put it back in my mouth again.

Jared and Libby and I are smoking grass.

September 1972

Libby and Jared meet me and some other friends at a
speech by Jane Fonda. The auditorium is filled beyond
capacity and it is very hot, still like summer. The public
address system isn't working well and I am sweating and
beginning to have what I know will be an anxiety attack.
I look at Libby sitting next to me: she is so serene. How
can she be that calm all the time unless she's stupid?

Sometimes Libby can say incredible things. When Jane
Fonda's talking about Cambodia, Libby leans over to
me and whispers, "Is Cambodia with us or against us?"
I shrug my shoulders. Jane Fonda goes on speaking
hoarsely. Jared falls asleep. Afterwards a group of us go
out to get something to eat.

Libby announces that over the summer she has become
a vegetarian. I order my hamburger anyway. Libby has a
bagel and then gets a terrible stomachache and I have to
drive her home. She is silent the whole trip. At her door
Jared kisses her goodnight. It is a casual kiss, almost
chaste, but then she isn't feeling well. "Call you
tomorrow," Libby tells Jared. Again I am envious, not
of them specifically, but of people like them, people
who can afford to be casual, to kiss almost chastely.

February 1973

Somehow just Libby and I have lunch at Campus
Corner together without anyone else around. I am
uncomfortable and have to search around for topics.

~ 69 ~

Libby isn't very smart. She talks about Jared's mother and how Jared's mother serves fish whenever Libby comes over for dinner, just because she knows Libby cannot stand the look of it.

"She even leaves the eyes in the fish," Libby tells me. I nod, make a face. I cannot stand the sight of fish, either.

Hamburgers are more up my alley because I don't have to think about cows.

August 1973

Libby has spent the summer going cross-country with my best friend Avis. In her letters Avis sometimes sends regards from Libby. After they get back from California, Avis has a party. Jared is still at camp being a water safety instructor, so Libby comes to the party with a chunky red-haired guy who Avis says is madly in love with Libby. He drives 170 miles from Pennsylvania every other weekend just to spend the day with Libby. I like the guy.

Later, after the party, Avis says about Libby: "I don't know how it happened: a nice Russian Orthodox girl from such a sheltered home suddenly got so promiscuous."

Of course Avis is not judging Libby; she says it in a matter-of-fact way, and I think that Avis considers herself promiscuous. I say nothing, just go on helping Avis wash the dishes.

December 1973

I have been in love with someone for almost a year. I feel completely secure. Libby and Jared are still together, of course.

February 1974

In the library I meet Libby, who is fretting over a speech she has to give in class. "Take deep breaths," I say.

"I'm afraid I'll hyperventilate," she says, laughing but full of fear. I laugh too.

I almost say "It's only a speech" but quickly realize what a stupid thing that would be to hear.

"How's Jared?" I say instead.

"Fine," Libby says.

 "How's your stomach these days?"

"Getting smaller. Feel." I put my palm on her abdomen.

"I wish I could lose weight like that," I say. "How'd you do it?"

"Aggravation."

"I've got the same problem, but that only makes me put it on..." Then I think: "Libby, we're graduating. I can't believe that you never took Speech before this."

"I wish I had."

I wonder if her teeth are chattering. She looks like a lost sparrow. Although it is something I almost never do, I put my arm around her shoulder and I squeeze her hand with my other hand.

Libby smiles.

The bell rings, and Libby's muscles tense.

"Knock 'em dead," I tell her as she walks unsteadily to class. I never do find out how her speech turns out.

June 1974

Libby invites me to a going-away party she is giving for Avis, who has decided to live in Israel following her graduation. I will miss Avis terribly, though we haven't been as close as we once were.

Libby is sharing an apartment with two guys and a woman. It is a dinner party, and Libby's mattress board held up by milk cartons is our table. I sit next to Avis's sister, who I know from high school, who shares interesting gossip with me. Jared is sitting on the other side of me, and I notice he does not look well. When Jared says he is leaving for camp on Thursday, I wonder how old he'll be when he'll stop being a counselor.

At the party I meet some nice new people and chat with some people I have known almost all my life. Leonard comes in from his apartment next door to use the telephone; his was taken out after he didn't pay the bill. Libby invites Leonard to stay to dinner. Avis tells him to stay. Everyone else agrees.

Jared sings some folk-rock as he plays his guitar. Dinner is vegetarian: eggplant parmigiana and some other stuff I cannot eat. But afterwards there is a cake for Avis with a joint on it instead of a candle.

The icing on the cake says the equivalent of "bon voyage" in Hebrew, or so Libby tells me, a Russian Orthodox girl telling a Jewish boy something he should already know. One of her roommates, the shirtless gay guy with the ponytail and great abs I keep staring at, baked the cake.

At the end of the night I hug Avis hard, tell her how much I'll miss her. Libby watches us.

"Maybe you can convince her to stay," Libby says to me.

"I can't convince anyone to do anything," I say back to Libby, still holding onto Avis, still staring at Libby's gay roommate, who knows seven languages.

"Poor Kevin," says Libby, and joins us in our hug.

December 1974

Everyone knows that Libby has left Jared for Leonard. I am noncommittal. I am no longer in love with anyone but sometimes I find myself feeling extraordinarily, unpredictably happy. I tell Jared he must stop moping around.

"Get out of your bedroom," I say to him. One afternoon he tells me Vicky has told him the same thing. As Leonard's discarded girlfriend, she is the other injured party in the matter. I try to become everyone's confidant.

Somehow it is decided that the three of us are going to a modern dance recital at the college: me, Jared and Vicky. A strange combination, but I ask three times if they are sure they want me to tag along and each time they say yes. I figure they figure other people will look at them strangely if they're seen together without someone else; people will think they're just seeing each other out of revenge. I make it look like they're in a group.

Jared and Vicky both still live with their parents, whose houses are two blocks apart. After the recital (I liked the part when the dancers unrolled toilet paper) we go to Vicky's house, where we sit in her bedroom, which is filled with so many plants I wonder they do not cut off her oxygen supply at night.

We talk about how incomprehensible most of the dance pieces were and I wonder if I'm not in the way. But I make no attempt to leave early, and Jared tells us he's going to see Libby tomorrow for the first time in two months. Vicky says, "That's like walking a tightrope backwards, isn't it, Kevin?"

I have to agree. Vicky looks sad when she talks about missing visiting Leonard's grandmother up at her farm in the country, but says she's determined to see other people and forget that she ever knew Leonard.

"I can't do that with Libby," Jared says, yawning. I think a few things but do not say them aloud.

March 1975

I run into Vicky at the shopping mall and we go have pizza together. "You look great," Vicky tells me.

"You too," I say.

"I'm seeing somebody," Vicky says. "A teacher. He's wonderful. We were out till five last night." I smile. I am glad for her. She says Leonard and she are in the same cinema class and he wonders why she treats him so coldly. He and Libby are not seeing each other anymore.

Vicky stirs her soda with the straw. "Have you seen Jared lately? He's still so hung up on Libby, following her around everywhere..."

"No, I've been keeping pretty much to myself."

Vicky laughs. Then suddenly she says: "You were in love with Avis, weren't you?"

"Possibly." That is not quite a lie.

"How's she doing in Israel?"

"She married someone on the kibbutz."

"No kidding!...But you're all right, aren't you?" I am so terribly touched by this woman, this almost-stranger, thinking of me.

"Of course," I chuckle. "I'm fine."

Vicky nods her head. "You and me, Kevin, we're survivors. Jared isn't. He'll never get over Libby. Can you figure out what he sees in her?" I think of Libby's face, her body, her laugh.

"No," I tell Vicky.

June 1975

Libby invites me to a party she is giving for Jared. So they are seeing one another again. But the night before the party, Jared stops by my house with another woman, another old friend from school, someone who later becomes a Sikh and moves to Espanola, New Mexico.

Maybe Jared's a survivor too, I think.

July 1975

I am taking Libby to a free gynecological clinic. She has asked me to accompany her, "not just because you have a car, but because you're the only one I could go with."

Jared is being a counselor at camp again. I am astounded when Libby tells me she has never seen a gynecologist before.

"How old are you?" I ask her, and I am again astounded to learn that Libby is six months older than I. All along I'd figured she was a couple of years younger.

The clinic is in a slum in Coney Island. It is depressing and my puns about "the miscarriage trade" and so on go over Libby's head. It is three hours before she is called. We are the only white people in the waiting room. I squeeze Libby's hand before she goes into the examining room.

I wait for what seems a very long time. A kid who doesn't look more than thirteen says to me, "Hey, man, you done knock up your fox?"

I tell him no. The time goes on and I have to go out and call Libby's boss to say that she will not be able to come into the store that night. He says it's all right, but says it in a way that means it's not all right.

Finally Libby comes out, looking very pale. She grabs my hand. Could it have been that bad? Either she has the infection or not. She didn't want Jared to know. Libby thinks Vicky is responsible for Jared giving her the infection; I know better, know about the other woman, but I will not say so. For once in my life I am being discreet.

Suddenly Libby is in my arms crying. People are staring at us, but I don't care. All afternoon I had been annoyed with Libby for making me come to this horrible place but now that doesn't matter. I am a man being held by a woman who needs him. Even if Libby and I are only friends, I am her protector. I have never protected anyone before.

"What's wrong? Is the infection bad?" I don't know anything about women's infections.

"Oh, I have pills for the infection, that's nothing...but the doctor said I have an ovarian cyst." She is crying even more. I take her out of the clinic, away from the staring faces. I do not know what an ovarian cyst is, but I do know that my aunt had one and had a fairly serious operation. "He wants me to take x-rays," Libby is sobbing. I feel so inadequate yet at the same time I am taking pleasure from the fact that it is me Libby is sharing this with and no one else.

I take her out to dinner and try like hell, working up a sweat, to make her stop crying and trembling. Finally I get a smile on her face. I kiss her.

December 1975

Christmas dinner at Libby's house: just me and her mother and her brother and Avis, who is visiting us from Israel. Libby's cyst does not have to be operated on yet, it seems. She has fallen in love again -- with Simon, an English guy.

When Jared came back from camp, he introduced Libby to his counselor friend Simon. Libby and Simon fell in love, and Jared is, in Libby's mother's words to me as we drink eggnog together in the kitchen, "eating his heart out once again." I am crazy about Libby's mother, who is as relaxed as my own mother is hard-edged. Libby's mother knows stuff about me that my own mother does not.

Jared looks terrible these days. Avis and I keep trying to get him to come to the movies with us, but he always makes some excuse. He doesn't know what to do with his life and has taken a job in a record store. There is no future in it, of course. He refuses to see Libby and we cannot mention Libby's name in his presence.

Libby gives me my Christmas present, a handkerchief. It is years since I have used a handkerchief, but I'm glad I have one now. I give Libby a pair of slippers with bunny rabbits on them. Libby says she loves them, and I believe her. Libby and I and her mother and brother and Avis sit around the table and stuff ourselves, fall asleep for a while, take a walk in the wet snow.

Avis tells us she is thinking about returning for good; her marriage hasn't worked out. Libby says Avis coming back to New York is ironic because she herself is going to England next month to stay with Simon. She has bought a 45-day ticket.

April 1976

"Libby? It's Kevin."

(I have not spoken to her since I picked her up from the airport in February. In England Simon asked her to marry him. She may do it.)

"...Lib, I don't know how to tell you this..."

(I heard it myself over the radio before another friend called.)

"Jared's brother – Wally – passed away. He killed himself. He jumped off the roof of the student center."

(Wally used to laugh when his mother served fish with the eyes still in it just to annoy Libby.)

"The funeral's tomorrow. Do you want to go?"

(She can't. She'd like to, she wants to, but she can't hurt Jared any more than he's hurt already. She'll send him a note.)

"I'm sorry to have had to tell you..."

(Why did I have to? Yet it was the first thing I thought of to do when I got home.)

September 1976

Jared comes over to my place. Being away for the summer agreed with him. As it did me. "Libby got your card," he tells me.

"I didn't know you were seeing Libby," I say. I don't like this. How come I didn't know?

"I was there last week.... We're sort of seeing each other, but we're seeing other people as well." I suggest we go take a drive to Libby's house.

When we get to her block we see her and Leonard playing frisbee in the street.

"It's Kevin!" she shouts, not even noticing Jared at first. Libby says she is glad to see me, and the four of us toss the frisbee for a while and then Libby and Leonard go out to dinner as they had planned.

Driving Jared home, I ask him, "Does it bother you, her seeing Leonard?"

"No," says Jared.

I will not see him for another year. In November he will move upstate. He and Libby will stay in close touch, but I will not hear much from either of them. I have my own empty life, thank you.

May 1977

Libby's mother calls me one night.

"I just wanted to let you know," her mother says. "Libby's going into the hospital for an operation. They found this cyst on her ovary the size of a grapefruit. She's very upset. Tonight her friend Ted took her to dinner so she's all right. But I thought you would want to know. She didn't want to tell you herself...."

May 1977

That night I dream of making love to Libby. In the morning I call her.

May 1977

It is the day before Libby's surgery. Her surgeon, a woman in her thirties who is charging only $300 for the operation, has just left. I am sitting by Libby's bed. So is Ted. Another Libby admirer--there are so many.

Libby makes everyone feel happy. There are so many presents in the room. I don't know why I bought her a Venus's flytrap, but I found it interesting and thought she might too. Ted has brought her an Andre Gide novel, in French. I can't imagine Libby understanding a word of it.

Libby seems cheerful enough. My bunny rabbit slippers – hers – are on the floor.

A man comes in with a consent form to sign. He explains that it absolves the surgeon of responsibility in

the event of something happening; for instance, if
Libby should become sterile after the operation....
"Sterile?" There is panic in Libby's eyes. Lamely, Ted
and I try to comfort her.

"My grandmother had to sign the same thing before her
cataract operation last year," I joke, but nobody gets it.

Ted doesn't do any better than me in the comforting
department. Visiting hours end too early. In the
elevator Ted tells me he's really worried. He's about 19,
snub-nosed, freckled, cute. He must be in love with
Libby.

May 1977

When they tie her down to the operating table, Libby
starts screaming. After the surgery, she is very weak.
She gets lots of visitors. Her mother, Ted and I come
every day. Other people come every other day. One
afternoon they tell her to take a walk and I am the only
one visiting her and we walk down the corridor to see
the newborn babies. One of them is connected to
machines that monitor every beat of her heart.

She's premature, Libby explains. The infant is bathed in
infrared light. I can't believe that's a life. Libby and I
watch the infant's heartbeat on the monitor and then
she feels tired and I assist her in walking back to her
room.

Ted and her mother are in the room when we get there.

~ 83 ~

July 1977

Avis is in from Israel again, maybe this time for good. Ted gets along with Avis, and the four of us sit around Libby's house. Libby's brother is complaining about no orange juice in the house. "Mom says we're boycotting because of Anita Bryant and the fags," he whines.

We ignore him and decide to go out to eat. Libby tells us she has been invited out to a commune in Washington State, where some of her friends live. She might go.

Avis says Libby's better off living permanently in the commune than in the neighborhood by her mother's house, which is still seedy. "That's a possibility," Libby says.

During a Szechuan dinner in Chinatown, I suddenly remember something and ask Libby whatever happened to that premature little girl in the hospital.

"Nothing," Libby says. "As far as I know, she got better and went home." I was expecting a different answer.

December 1977

Another Christmas at Libby's mother's house. We are like a family now, Libby and her mother and her brother and his girlfriend and Ted and I. As I look across the table at Ted, he smiles at me and I feel very grateful for Libby's ovarian cyst.

("Why didn't you tell me, you guys?" Libby had said excitedly and hugged both of us, but I'm sure she knew.)

Jared is with us this Christmas, visiting too. He and Libby still make love. I am glad about that.

(After Libby's plane took off for Seattle, Ted and I walked back to the parking lot and found my car had a flat. That was the night I kissed him for the first time. Ted said he'd been waiting for me to do something for months.)

In the kitchen, putting dishes in the sink, Libby's mother says to me: "My daughter never gave me one moment's trouble." I can't imagine too many mothers saying that about their children. Not mine, certainly. My mother is kind of annoyed with me right now.

(In two days Libby will be going back to Washington State, taking a Greyhound bus to live with the man who has fallen in love with her. He has a place right next to her friends' commune.)

We lie around the house, full of food, full of Christmas, singing along as Jared strums his guitar.

(Can it be more than six years that I know Libby?)

June 1978

Hello Kevin,

Please don't be upset at me, though I haven't written you've been on my mind and on my tongue often. In fact I had to explain you to Kieran -- I talked of you so much was wondering what you were to me. I haven't been to the city very much lately. The weather's been too nice. And for the past couple of weeks we've had friends come for the weekend and we've been having picnics. I made all sorts of food & even a strawberry cream pie -- I picked the strawberries the day before.

Berrypicking is great -- I've never done it on such a large scale. We have 3 rasp. bushes in the backyard. I really get off on the picking -- the berries are a hundreds times better than those in the stores -- I've been back there picking many times -- they also have blueberries and boysenberries, all less than a mile away. I planted several vegetables but the deer and rabbits had a feast. They left the garlic and onions -- but have just started attacking them this week. What really upset me was that they even ate all my plants, even my sunflowers. That just wasn't very nice.

Life here is still the same. I clean, sew, cook, bake, weave and eat too much. I've been on a diet for the past two days. Kieran laughs at me and says I'm beginning to get his stomach. Kieran's still working as a framer building houses. He plans to work until the end of Sept. and then we're off to L.A. for the winter. Kieran's love-goal is to write songs (words) for a living. He works best with his friend Howie in L.A. -- have I told you this already?

Well anyway he'll go down there to help move his tunes around -- people are interested and he's going to see it through. I'm not very excited about moving to L.A. but I'll try it. It won't be for very long anyway. We'll be back here in the spring. I've been hearing from Avis and also Jared -- all seems OK with them both. I was happy to hear Jared got the teaching job. Have you seen Mom lately? I know how much she likes having you drop by. Ted did write me from France. I guess he writes you too. The religious conference went really well, he said. Did he write you about wanting to stay in Europe longer? He seems content there. Do you miss him a lot?

Well I must be getting to work. I'm surprising Kieran with a cherry pie. I've never made one before. Take care of yourself and don't be like me – write soon.

Love ya
XXXO
Libby

Unobtrusive Methods,
Inchoate Designs

Kevin tried to remember just who it was in his dusty past that was fond of saying, "Let's look at reality." It was either Mrs. Slane, the cleaning woman whom he had bitten on the elbow as a child, or Dr. Kiremdijian, the botany professor at college. But of course there was always the possibility that it might have been Eric, Eric in one of his playful moments when he was imitating some pompous professor.

Eric, of course, never had said anything, since Eric was only a name Kevin had given to a boy he had once seen and wanted to talk to in Washington Square Park on a Good Friday that was much too hot for anything proper. Eric – it was two weeks later that Kevin decided to call him Eric – was standing just on the fringe of the body of the park, not in the inner core of the peopled fountain nor in the next ring containing the benches, but off to one side, leaning against the unmovable arch, staring at everything except Kevin.

Kevin himself stood off to a corner, near some frisbee players, watching the boy he would later call Eric. Kevin took it all in: the dark ringlets of hair, the faint bead of perspiration on the brow and smooth upper lip, the veins of the upper arm, smoothly muscled yet somehow delicate, the mustard-yellow T-shirt that said *The Little Prince*, advertising the old movie version of the Antoine de Saint-Exupéry fantasy, the shorts, jeans cut off at least seven inches above the knee, the long slim legs sprinkled with blondish hairs, the soiled white Keds his ankles had been poured into. Kevin took this all in and somewhere it registered that there was a reality that was the boy, and there was a reality that was called Eric, and there was also a reality for Kevin in which she had created the fantasy wherein Eric was the one fond of saying, "Let's look at reality" – or indeed, in which Eric existed at all.

One time Kevin asked Dr. Kiremedjian in the campus coffee shop whether a man's character was his fate or whether a man's fate was his character. Dr. Kiremdjian protested that he was only a botanist and smiled wanly, but when Kevin pressed him, Dr. Kiremdjian ventured his opinion that character and fate were separate and non-contiguous entities – very much like Kevin and Eric, or Kevin and the cleaning woman, or Kevin and himself, Dr. Kiremdjian.

None of them touched any other except in their respective imaginings, and the characters they were, being mere products of individual minds, were thus not consistent. Kevin's Eric was an eighteen-year-old high school senior, for example; but Mrs. Slane's Eric was a forty-year-old electrician; and the Eric that Dr. Kiremdjian had created was not even a person at all, but a plant – a leafy rhododendron who responded gaily to the music of Ravel.

That Dr. Kiremdjian was a botanist and Mrs. Slane a cleaning woman and Kevin an agnostic determined their respective personal compositions. One could not put Mrs. Slane's Kevin, for instance, in a room with Kevin's Dr. Kiremdjian; some unspoken law of quantum physics precluded any possibility of that. So ultimately no one's reality could be looked upon as real for anyone else, since every person was a fiction created by another, except in cases where the relationship had never existed in the first place – i.e., Mrs. Slane had never encountered in her thoughts the character of a botany professor named Dr. Kiremdjian.

Seen in this light, the nameless boy in Washington Square Park could be the most or least real of all – the qualifiers

~ 89 ~

"most" and "least" when applied to "real" being of dubious significance in the framework of this story.

Or to look at it another way: An elderly black man on a hot Good Friday 1975 in Washington Square Park asks four people in turn for a dime with which he can gather enough money to purchase a bottle of wine, explaining to them, "Nothin' to do but buy me some wine, which'll at least let me feel good for a couple of hours."

This all his reality, and the four people he has approached and from whom he has received change include the preceding characters in this story: Kevin, Mrs. Slane, Dr. Kiremdjian, and the boy Eric, each of them being merely a fictitious representation in the mind of the elderly wino. So if we are to assume that reality is seen through the wino's eyes, then story of Kevin's apprehension of the boy Eric perhaps begins to make sense, for through the gray haze of an alcoholic vision on a darkening hot Good Friday, Kevin's is only one of an infinite number of possible realities.

Therefore we may conclude that it is up to each of us to create our own characters, our own stories, our own realities, and not depend upon others for our fictions. The elderly wino knows this. Kevin, Mrs. Slane, Dr. Kiremdjian, and the boy Kevin has called Eric do not understand this as yet, although if by chance they happen to stumble on this story, they may eventually discover, affirm, and appreciate the reality of their own existence.

Understanding Human Sexual Inadequacy

Kevin is staring at a notice in the library when someone pinches him from behind. It is Michelle Fell, this girl in his Poli Sci class. She's really ugly but has the biggest tits Kevin has ever seen. He thinks she's got a crush on him.

Shelli and Kevin have sex in his room and it is cool. Then Elspeth comes over and they all go swimming. Elspeth isn't sleeping with anyone, so she's stopped taking the Pill. She confides to her friends that she slept with two other guys while she was engaged to Jerry.

Elspeth bursts in with news of a phone call from Carole last night. Carole said Izzy asked her to marry him, but she didn't know if he loved or if it was "just because everything we've been through – losing the baby and all…" "What?" Elspeth said. Carole was four weeks late with her period when she fell down a flight of stairs. She was in a very bad way and the doctor said she had had a miscarriage. He gave her a saline solution shot. Elspeth tells Kevin she has won this month's prize for the best gossip.

Kevin is preoccupied during a Poli Sci lecture and also at lunch with Shelli and Elspeth. Carol and Izzy were using condoms too, he thinks, and look what happened to them. Shelli isn't due for her period for another week or so, but she told Kevin that they will see a gynecologist. Damn it, he did not want to be a father.

Mark and Consuelo tell Kevin that in the beginning every couple goes through this. Anyway, if Shelli is pregnant, Mark says, he can get Father Reagan to marry them.

Shelli and Kevin go to see *Love Story*. Very shallow, Kevin thinks. By the end of the movie everyone around them is in tears. Kevin is surprised to look over and see Shelli's wet cheeks. Then he finally gets around to crying himself.

Shelli makes a beautiful maid of honor for her sister Louise. She catches the bouquet. Kevin is fidgety and uncomfortable during the wedding, but he forces himself to stay there until it ends.

Shelli cries because she will miss her sister. She and Kevin make love and the orgasms reaffirm their devotion. They also relax both of them.

Summer school is a bore, so Kevin and Shelli cut class, take a cab home, go to Kevin's bedroom, watch *Sesame Street*, and eventually make love. Kevin can't capture on paper the ecstasy of loving that girl. Suffice it to say that she's really terrific.

Finding the campus deserted, Kevin and Shelli go home, read the *Voice*, read the *Times*, read *The National Lampoon*. They laugh at a comic in which someone calls Adlai Stevenson "Fuckface." They also get into bed and have an exquisite time.

Kevin wonders if Shelli's feeling guilty about sex. He doesn't think *he* does. Shelli's new shrink, Dr. Russell, says she's attracted to Kevin because she can mother him. Anyway, Kevin thinks, Shelli seems to be getting better at it.

Kevin is driving home when she suddenly says, "I'm getting hold." He laughs, but later he begins to realize what she meant.

After their Patty Melts for lunch at the International House of Pancakes, Kevin and Shelli go shopping and come back home. They make love and lie naked in bed, talking for an hour. It'll be a great relief when her period comes.

When Kevin gets on campus, Shelli comes by, looking very upset. She confesses to Kevin and Elspeth that she did not sleep because she was worried about her period being late. She goes into the ladies' room to check, as Elspeth tries to console Kevin – in Elspeth's way, which is to say not at all. She is in there a long time and Kevin grows hopeful, but Shelli comes out saying she was in there so long helping Alice look for a lost contact.

The minute they get home, Shelli goes to the bathroom and finds out she is menstruating. They are both joyous and relieved. The day turns remarkably bright and beautiful. They have lunch at Burger King and then go to the mall. Kevin buys a furry creature, pineapple incense, a book, and a glass bottle.

They have a fight, and Shelli walks out, but twenty minutes later she comes back.

Shelli calls Kevin at 9 a.m., a few minutes after he's gotten up. "Guess what?" she says. "What?" Kevin says, and Shelli replies. "I got my period this morning!" She made up the whole thing yesterday to spare him from worry. All day she was just pretending. She tells him that if she didn't get it, she was going to get an abortion with Elspeth and not tell him. Shelli must love Kevin a lot to do something like that.

Shelli's friends come over to the pool. Stacy is about the butchest girl Kevin has ever met. She's attracted to him, he can feel it. When Stacy tells him he looks like he's from California, Kevin gets a hard-on. Meanwhile, Shelli is upstairs, sick with her period.

Shelli is hurt that Brian has gone to be a counselor at a summer camp and left without saying goodbye. Brian is a supreme moralist, Kevin thinks. When Brian found out that Shelli and Kevin were having an affair, he practically stopped being her friend. Kevin writes Brian a nasty letter.

They make love – in a fashion, since Shelli still has her period. Then he writes a term paper for her, comparing Joyce's *Portrait of the Artist* with Cleaver's *Soul on Ice*.

She makes him feel so wonderful when she says he is so sexy. Kevin is a bit of a narcissist. When they make love, it is even more beautiful. Just when Kevin thinks their relationship is in trouble, he comes to the realization that he loves her so goddam much. Those looks she gives him: her crooked baby-smile, her disbelieving gaze, her open and pure look. He could store them in a file in his mind.

When Elspeth tells her mother she wants to move out and live with Mark and Consuelo, her mother gets angry. "If you do that," Elspeth's mother says, "I won't speak to you anymore." Elspeth says this would lead to her having a nervous breakdown, so she's not doing it.

Kevin drives Shelli to the orthodontist and goes to eat lunch and read. He picks her up an hour later and sees her braces back on. They go home to bed, and what joy that is. They don't even have one fight, except Shelli complains about leaving so early.

Shelli's shrink tells her she should date other guys. This is after Shelli told Dr. Russell that Kevin's shrink told him he should date other girls. Kevin gets to thinking maybe the shrinks are right: they *are* clinging to each other neurotically. So he tells her she can date other guys. Shelli hangs up crying.

They kiss and they cry. She gives him a card that says, "I don't love you because I need you. I need you because I love you." There is a sunset on the front of it.

Kevin gets a postcard from Jerry from Switzerland. Jerry writes: "There is still a great struggle going on within me, a struggle symbolized by inability to reconcile Gide's thrust for life with Camus's struggle for justice." Elspeth looks at the postcard and says that's one of the reasons she broke up with Jerry. Also he wasn't that good in bed.

Shelli gets a phone call from a guy she met in the bookstore the day before. He is a friend from high school. He asks Shelli to go to the beach with him. It hurts her to hurt the guy, but she says she can't and gently works into the conversation that she has a boyfriend. Kevin tells her that maybe should have gone out with the guy.

In bed, Shelli tearfully confesses something to Kevin: that just before Jerry went to Europe, when they visited him and Kevin had to leave early to study, Jerry lay on the bed with her with his arm around her. Jerry told her not to tell Kevin, that it would hurt him. Kevin tells Shelli it is no big deal.

Kevin comes much too quickly. It would not be so bad but he can't get a hard-on afterwards.

They play Monopoly with the teddy bear and drink two cans of Hawaiian Punch each. Then they make love and it is beautiful.

An Appropriated Story

My protagonists are the fragments of a memory. They are the only ones you may trust.

©

My whole wheat bread is weeping. Crying silently. Even now. As I hold the sandwich in my hands, my pudgy architect's hands. Lorna must have put too much liebestod in the batter. Otherwise why would it cry? With each bite, the tears grow less, and they are muted inside of me. Each bread-tear takes that no-frills journey down my esophagus, into the central cavity that is my stomach, their river Lethe. On the television, guns are being fired. An old movie replayed: *Each Dawn I Die*.

"Is that with John Garfield?" I ask Martin.

Martin is annoyed with me. Without changing his expression, he gives a look of disapproval and says, "No. James Cagney."

"We are all eight-year-olds with earaches," somebody says.

©

I awake two seconds after midnight. The pain has gotten much worse. I can hardly move my head, and when I try to move my head, there are paroxysms so great that I must moan without wanting to.

All night I am like that.

I hear Lorna cry out, "What's the matter?" from the room next door. But I say, "Go back to sleep."

Somehow I sleep. But my dreams are all of pain. In one, Martin refuses to believe that my neck hurts as much as it does.

When I awake in the morning, the situation goes back to what it had been the evening before, when the tuxedos were out and the fountain full of soap suds. It is back to what it was. A twinge, a feeling that something had snapped and needed only to solidify again.

But I can move around with greater comfort.

©

The Book of Revelations is misplaced, there at the end of the New Testament. It should be in the Old Testament, or in the Apocrypha at least.

I finally realize that Lorna does not want to look at me. I ask Martin to read the letter I received during the January thaw, to see what Martin thinks.

He reads the letter without his glasses. Martin announces that the letter is matter-of-fact. He looks down at the parson's table and says, "It sounds like she's straining for things to say."

I am too close to the situation.

~ 99 ~

"Maybe Lorna will be at the airport in New Amsterdam," Martin says.

"And maybe there's an Easter bunny, too."

I have the anger of disillusionment, but as Martin says, it's my own doing. Always. I have been working since fall, working and planning, and now it is here and there's nothing. I'm busy. I've stopped running to the mailbox. I've been gathering myself together, preparing for the worst in New Amsterdam.

A strange woman, an old alcoholic nurse with baggy eyes, comes into my room and takes my hand. "Maybe it's better to let it out now," she says.

"No," I tell her. "I'll control myself until I get there. I will not break down until I see her. Or don't see her, as the case may be."

Three Elavils, several thousand miles and a bolt of lightning later, I am there. Lorna is waiting.

©

She kisses me, a rerun of that New Amsterdam kiss. I can feel that her throat is sore.

Lorna has been singing three hours for friends who may go to Canada with her this summer. She tells me, perhaps facetiously, that she hopes I can get together with her friends someday.

She asks how I am.

"Right now I'm rather confused," I say. "Things are happening too quickly for me to come to terms with them all. Although I've been doing nothing if not trying."

Lorna says that she'll say awhile; she'll stay until it's time for her to go.

©

Martin's girlfriend, the new one with the nose, the one whose name I cannot remember, phones us. I tell her that Martin is out playing cards.

Martin's girlfriend giggles.

"At least that's what he told me," I add.

A short silence, a principal holding up his hand in assembly. "Yeah," she says. "Well... I don't know if he's talking to me."

"Oh," I say. "Well then, should I tell him you called?"

"You can if you want to."

The story of my life.

"Okay," I say, and I think that the word comes from 'Old Kinderhook,' the nickname for Martin Van Buren. And I think of our Martin, who is supposed to be playing cards.

"Do you know anything?" Martin's girlfriend asks me.

"I'm a high school graduate," I tell her. "So I know *some* things."

Martin's girlfriend giggles and hangs up without saying goodbye.

©

"In high school everyone used to wonder about you," Lorna tells me.

Did they? Why didn't know that?

"But they were all wrong," she says. "You're a man."

There is freeze-dried coffee on the table, but neither of us will drink it. We talk of our generation, who is in law school and stuff:

"Still, you can't blame her."

"Even if he's not important to her anymore?"

"But on the other hand, she can't help feeling abandoned."

"He's married, and a paraplegic to boot."

"They're still talking of marriage even if they do bicker somewhat."

"She's found another man."

"They waited on line for Springsteen for hours."

"It probably won't happen until the end of summer."

Martin came down the stairs, and our conversation ended. Lorna gave him a wary smile. He had a book

with him, and he drank our coffee, and he sat with us
and recited words borrowed from Arabic:

"Saffron….mattress….cotton….safari….henna….
assassin….algebra….alcohol….arsenal….hashish….
gazelle….lemon….albatross…."

For Martin, it is a cinch.

©

"Like…" everyone says. The unfinished simile.

There is a person living in the State of Ohio, County of
Franklin, who to this day believes she has ruined my
life.

Like, she did….for a while. She had one of those Jane
Wyatt deliciously sweet but vicious characters. She
believed in fate. And her fate was to ruin my life.

For months I did not leave my room.   A nurse was
assigned to me. My car made a funny noise. My acne
flared up again. I screamed obscenities out the window.
I had strange thoughts. Radios made me cry.

But I got over it. Somehow. I learned to trust the
strange thoughts, to metamorphose them with a finality
I had barely suspected of existing.

And my life was not ruined. Once, at a wedding, an old
maid cousin told the bride in her dressing-room:
"Nobody ruins anybody else's life anymore. They don't
even want to try."

This person tried. But unlike Lorna, she could not
succeed.

~ 103 ~

©

One day I discovered Lorna's secret, quite by accident. I was on a Greyhound bus going to Philadelphia. Two elderly black churchwomen were sitting in the seats just in front of me. The one near the window was deaf, and her companion had to speak loudly and clearly. They couldn't have realized I was behind them because I was using Martin's ticket; the ticket had Martin's name on it, not mine. Martin was with his girlfriend, the nosy one, at my house. They were indeed trying to get rid of me, but I didn't care. Because on that bus ride I learned Lorna's secret. The non-deaf black old lady said:

"She done it 'cause she a fool!"

After that, it didn't bother me so much. It had nothing to do with me, in a way. I had done my best; I had behaved decently. Politely. I had never given Lorna a hard time. I never raised my hand to her as I had with Martin or the others. It was all Lorna's doing. Because she was a fool. *Is* a fool.

I sank back into my seat in the last row of the bus, leaving the driving to others. For the first time in weeks, I began to feel hungry. In the travel bag that Martin packed, there was a sandwich. His girlfriend had made it for me.

I took it out of the Ziploc bag. It was peanut butter and marshmallow fluff, on whole wheat bread that did not cry. By the time we got to Philadelphia, it was gone.

Rampant Burping

1

"Can you live with it?" the Army psychiatrist asked him at his draft physical.

He smiled expansively. "Now that I've discovered Andre Gide," he said, "I can live with *anything*."

2

Mother predicted Senator Dirksen's death one or two weeks before he died. I would say that a small clue was involved: Mother has exceptionally good perception and power of deduction when health is involved. It's almost as though she can "feel the patient out." She probably noticed the Senator's countenance growing worse, a certain quality in his voice, which might be a subtle hint of lung cancer, etc. Yes, this E.S.P. is difficult to understand, and at times it's hard to live with.

3

I am enclosing brief notes about myself hoping that they will serve the purposes for which you asked them; also a detail of the responsibilities of mayor. In case you someday become one, let me know to rejoice with you.

4

I opened the refrigerator this morning to find it empty.
I can't afford to feed Fayerweather Hall. Seriously, I
thought it would be a nice gesture to buy oranges,
apples, etc., in case we wanted them occasionally. And
now they're gone—and I heard you goned them!

5

Grandma disagreed with me about the war, but as
Grandpa said, "What does she know?"

6

"Is Rabbi Feldman there?" the caller asked. She
sounded old. It was a wrong number.

"He's dead," I said, and quickly hung up.

7

It's fully three years since he's "come out of it" and he'll
never go back.

8

Before it slips away, my middle name is Bruce; this was
my grandmother's choice.

The clothes we wear down here are the same as those
up your way. Sunglasses are of every type, likewise.

9

When people ask me what I plan to be after college, I
generally say I want to be a governess for a big family in
Spain. Sort of an Iberian Julie Andrews. But I still
have some secret thoughts about becoming a movie
critic. Ever since I saw a Peck & Peck ad in the Sunday
Times: "There's a certain kind of woman who thinks
that Renata Adler's job is like getting paid to eat
truffles…"

I should have realized at the time that it's sort of hard
to get in when they only take ten girls out of two
hundred.

10

We had most main things.

The only thing we did not have was the marathon-hunt.

11

Jamaica is lovely, but I prefer Aruba at Chanukah time.
'Chanukah' has several spellings in the dictionary; I
don't know if any spelling is used more than any other,
but I picked this one. Christina is too sensible and
spiritual for all this.

12

We have the right to be free from an arbitrary and capricious enforcement of a code of conduct.

We have other rights, too: twenty-three in all. The others are enumerated elsewhere.

13

Mrs. Frelinghuysen said it seemed to her that I wanted to 'luxuriate' myself in people, and I sarcastically said, "Fine. So I'll go to an orgy." But I know it's true. I see that lurking beneath that is another set of feelings, which make me need a variety of people. It's like an old Chinese puzzle box, and I'm afraid to see what's in the final box.

I had dinner last night at Burgerland. There was another customer there, a young man, and there were two waitresses, and both of us flirted with one of them. I realized that lurking in my mind was the feeling that we all go to bed together.

No wonder I have colitis.

14

Chicken in the car, car can't go: that's how you spell Chicago.

15

At Houston Street and the Bowery an old drunk comes
up to my car and wipes the windshield with a snotty
rag. He is toothless and smiling.

I give him a dime. As we drive away, Christina says I
should have given him a quarter.

16

He went into the little room where they would check
his hearing. He put on the earphones, but his
claustrophobia and the fact that he was unused to
wearing so much cologne combined to make him very
nauseous.

He stuck his finger down his throat, opened the door to
the little room and threw up on the sergeant.

"*What the fuck?*" the sergeant said.

17

Walking along the river, a jogging blonde girl passed us,
her breasts jiggling up and down, up and down.

"I admire girls who jog," I said.

The boy on my right looked at me. "I wonder why," he
said.

17a

Later, walking up Broadway, the boy on my right
stopped in a drug store to buy some Lectra-Shave. He
was no longer on my right.

The boy on my left pointed to a sign in the drug store
window: "K-Y Jelly, Reg. $1.29. Now 69¢"

"It's all cosmic," the boy on my left said.

17b

Much later, after dinner in fact, we cut across the
campus. The boy on my left (who had previously, by
the river, been the boy on my right) came up with an
idea. His idea was that the Miss America pageant be
staged on the steps of Low Library. Five contestants
could come out behind each of the ten pillars, and Bert
parks could sit on the lap of the statue of Alma Mater.

"Alma Mater," I repeated to myself.

18

It's so damn hot in this hotel room. It must've been a
hundred degrees every day I've been in Rome. There
are cockroaches in my room. I'm thirsty and out of
Liebfraumilch. In the room next door they're watching
television, it's "The Forsyte Saga," the episode with the
party, and Soames is telling the woman to shut up.

It would be shitty if she died while I was away. She was
a drug addict, a sick woman, but the first few years
(before diet pills) were quite good.

19

Christina's hymen is unbreakable. We've tried
everything: hammers, ice-picks, loose-leaf hole
punchers, pneumatic drills. Nothing works.

20

We had most main things.

The only thing that we did not have was the color war.

21

At the last Safari Awards, the last one ever, I went up to
accept the Worst Supporting Actress award for Anne
Wiazemsky. It was the third year in arrow that she'd
won it. That year, the award was a cut-out of the head
of 'Scoop' Jackson surrounded by sparklers.

I had the hiccups and had trouble speaking. People
laughed at me. He was kind and stepped in and told
another story about his draft physical.

The Army doctors asked him what he meant when he
checked 'stomach disorders' on the list of things wrong
with him. They wanted to know what kind of stomach
disorder he had.

He thought very quickly, back to the time when he was
nine years old and had eaten a whole salami and
couldn't stop belching for two days.

"I'm subject to fits of rampant burping," he told them.

Talking to a Stranger

"Did you have a very happy… somewhat happy… somewhat unhappy… very unhappy… childhood?" Ronna asks me.

"Oh, let's say 'somewhat unhappy,'" I tell her.

Ronna's mother is in survey research. We help her out by manufacturing interviews. Ronna's mother gives us each some of the money she earns. Ronna and I take turns being different subjects. This particular interview was commissioned by some sociologists at the University of Chicago. This is my first time with it, so I am playing myself.

"Do you consider yourself," Ronna asks, "very independent… somewhat independent… somewhat dependent… very dependent?"

I laugh my high-pitched laugh. "After two years," I ask her, "can't you answer that one by yourself?"

*

I have an anxiety dream. In it, I am late for my comprehensive exam. I see the clock on the wall of my kitchen, and I try to run to the college, but I cannot make it in time, something keeps slowing me down.

I wake up in a cold sweat, with a headache from studying too much.

*

Alice is leaving her job as secretary to the student government in order to attend fashion school. I know someone, an old girlfriend of Joshua's, who goes to the same school. Joshua met her in the hospital when his aunt was ill. The girl was in the hospital because she'd swallowed seventy-one aspirins in a suicide attempt. Months later, the girl was about to jump off the roof of the building housing the fashion school when a boy who looked exactly like Joshua came over to her. At first she thought it was Joshua but this boy said his name was Logan and he offered her a joint. She didn't jump.

*

The phone wakes me. It is Ronna singing a song from her favorite musical: *"It's Maaay, it's Maaay, the luus-sty month of Maaay."* All I can think of is that in a month it will all be over.

*

In high school Spanish class, I learned about Cinco de Mayo. At some point in my life, I decided to throw a penny into the bay each year on Cinco de Mayo, just for good luck. I haven't missed a year since.

*

The student government elections are on again. Everyone is ripping everyone else's campaign posters down. This is called "sniping." Elections never change.

*

Joshua tells me he think he is ready for a relationship, "either meaningful or meaningless."

*

Fay cannot help making sarcastic remarks about Dinnerstein and his new girlfriend. It infuriates her that they plan to say they are married and live in the married students' dorm. "They're hypocrites!" she howls as she prepares for her own wedding next month. Fay left Dinnerstein for Mitchell, his best friend, whom she thinks is not a hypocrite.

*

All this studying has left a bedraggled taste in my mouth. I went to visit Grandpa Ike, and he showed me the latest of his nail and string designs. This one was intertwined American and Israeli flags on a background of black velvet, with the word *Shalom* written in nail-and-string Hebrew.

*

Alice puts out *Matilda*, her newspaper for little old Jewish ladies. It is named for her late grandmother. *Matilda* features recipes, household hints, an advice column (Alice makes up the questions as well as the answers), fashion news, tips on staying slim and svelte, and quotes about women from people like Bulwer-Lytton. Ever since we were kids, Alice's perspicacity has never ceased to amaze.

*

My mother says, "I hope you left the bathroom clean; that's all I care about."

*

All this studying is driving me mad. I'll probably end up like Sidney, who finds Freudian significance even in *Matilda.*

*

Joshua has found a girl. "I lust after her," he says. She is a beautiful blonde who thinks she's a witch.

*

"Two steps forward and how many back?" Dr. McKenzie-Smith asks. No doubt she is right.

*

"I'll be leaving soon," I tell my father.

"What time will you be back?" he asks.

"I don't mean tonight," I say. "I mean forever."

*

I think of questions they can ask me on my comprehensive. Like "Relate the concept of Wyrd in *Beowulf* to Mark Twain's idea of luck in *Huckleberry Finn.*"

*

Question: Is it better for people to be dead to one another if they cause each other pain when they see each other?

*

The student government elections are over. In his victory speech, the new student government president threatens to put an ax through the college president's door.

There is a victory party in the Student Center. Alice leaves early, after someone spills wine on her blouse. That night Alice and Ronna and Fay go to Someplace New. Even though she is graduating, Ronna is going to Someplace New for the first time. Prior to this she'd told people, "I'm not the Someplace New type." But she seems to fit in all right.

Fay gets a little drunk on apple wine. She makes a nasty remark about Dinnerstein: "He's just going to law school because he doesn't want to face fucking reality."

"You're being bitter," Alice cautions her.

"You bet I am," Fay says.

*

I take a break from studying and go out for Carvel with Sidney. He always says he wears a yarmulke because he's proud of being Jewish. Freud didn't wear a yarmulke, I tell him. Sidney gives me a dirty look.

*

I've been living, breathing *Doctor Faustus* and Jane Austen.

*

Before the test, I am nervous. I get a haircut and go to see Dr. McKenzie-Smith. "You're a prime example of the ostrich syndrome," she tells me.

*

On the morning of the test, I get a note from Ronna. "I'll play Virginia Graham to your F. Scott Fitzgerald," she writes. *Beloved Infidel* must have been on TV recently. But who is *Virginia* Graham? Ronna certainly should know better.

*

1. Discuss the disintegration of civilization as seen in "The Waste Land" and "The Second Coming."

2. Compare Emma Bovary and Stephen Dedalus as romantics.

3. Who is the hero of *Paradise Lost?*

And so on.

*

After the test, I find another note from Ronna. "If you're going to be a master," this one says, "does that make me a mistress?"

*

I do not enjoy the John Denver concert. I am still worried about how I did on my exam. Professor Kramer walked into the room while I was taking the test and sadistically asked if the questions were hard enough. I know he hates me. He said he made up some of the questions, even though I specifically asked the department chairman to have two other teachers devise the exam. Perhaps Professor Kramer lied. After my hassle with him last term, I believe he is psychotic and capable of anything.

"Far-out!" Ronna keeps saying. I do not like John Denver; he keeps talking about how much he loves his wife. I think he protests too much. Besides, I have a terrible toothache.

Ronna and Alice talk about the concert on the ride home. I am in pain from my toothache. I do not feel on the same wavelength as Ronna. I don't say anything while I'm driving, except when I nearly run over a cat. Then I say, "Fucking cat!" with great intensity, and Ronna and Alice finally stop their ridiculous talking.

I drop Alice off first. Then I take Ronna home, kiss her on the cheek, don't say a word.

When I get home I look in the mirror and find out the reason for my toothache: one of my feelings has washed away.

*

"Your Freudian slip is showing," says Dr. McKenzie-Smith. She reminds me that at our last session I told her I hadn't been to a dentist in four years. "They start

trouble when they poke around in there," I had told
her. She gives me that tight little knowing smile.

*

I go to Grandma Bess's for lunch. She says I have
gotten thin. I only wish that were true.

If I eat the salad, Grandma says, "Why aren't you eating
the sandwich?" If I eat the sandwich, Grandma says,
"Don't you like the salad?"

Grandma asks me when Ronna and I are getting
married. I tell her I'm never going to get married. She
looks displeased and sighs.

"Oh, well," Grandma Bess says philosophically. "I'd
rather have you remain single than take those drugs."

*

Grandma Bess tells me about her father. He was a
good-looking man and felt his good looks entitled him
to a life of leisure, so he stayed at home sleeping all day
while his wife and mother-in-law went out and worked.

*

Ronna's mother tells her, "Don't you realize that every
third time you see him you end up crying?"

Ronna tells me this. We decide that neither of us wants
our relationship to continue the way it's been going.
We make a decision.

We will skip every third date.

*

Dr. Field inquires about "our mutual friend." He means my old girlfriend, his old patient. I tell Dr. Field that she is doing fine, even though I have heard she's psychotic and miserable. I don't want to hurt his feelings.

Afterwards he does a few magic tricks for me and Sidney.

*

Alice says she's in love with Mr. Blomberg. He was our old Spanish teacher, the one who taught me about Cinco de Mayo. But high school was years ago, I tell Alice.

Alice went back to the high school to see Mr. Blomberg, to find out when his drawings would be on display on the Promenade. Mr. Blomberg was teaching a class and told her to come back another day.

Ronna and I advise Alice to find out Mr. Blomberg's true feelings for her.

Alice is disgusted with Richie, her boyfriend. She says, "Richie and I never go anywhere or dress up and we always end up eating spaghetti on some curb or waiting to get thrown out of the lobby of the Plaza."

Alice says that after she dies, and I get her diaries, I'll learn that Richie was the cause of all her depressions. And all her highs as well.

Alice assumes that I'll outlive her because I am seven months younger than she. But she has forgotten that women live longer than men. I wonder what Alice will learn from my posthumous diaries.

*

It's getting warmer. I sat out in the sun for a while.

*

An old friend of Joshua's jumped off the roof of one of the apartment buildings in Trump Village. Joshua says he was a bit of a schlemiel, always on the verge of a nervous breakdown.

He jumped off the roof because the girl he'd been living with left him. Joshua says she was fat and not very pretty.

He might have slipped, Joshua thinks. When the television cameras came, he was heard to remark, "I'm on film now; it's okay."

Those were his last words.

*

Some old loony in Chock Full O' Nuts refuses to pay. I exchange bemused smiles with a blonde in a sweatshirt.

"It's *amused*, not *bemused*," Sidney tells me when I relate the incident. "*Bemused* means *fatchatted, verkempt*, confused. You're getting a masters degree in English?"

"Are you sure *bemused* means that?"

"Yeah," Sidney says, "and you use *enervated* wrong too."

I am both enervated and bemused, it turns out.

*

Joshua and I are at the UN, trying to film a
demonstration protesting an Arab massacre of Israeli
schoolchildren. Joshua has to hand in a final for his
Cinematography course and figures the UN
demonstration might be interesting.

There are a lot of yarmulkes and girls wearing stockings.
Perhaps Sidney is somewhere in the crowd.

Joshua says all Jewish girls are ugly. He says it softly
because there are Jewish girls crowding us from all
sides. He leans over to me and whispers, "If these were
WASPs, man, we'd be having a fucking orgy."

*

Cousin Missy has just come back from a Marriage
Encounter weekend. She is bubbling over with
excitement.

"You can't imagine what good things came of it," she
tells me. "Phil and I have finally decided to get a
divorce."

*

Now I have to worry about term papers. I haven't
gone to the department chairman yet to see how I did
on my comprehensive exam.

*

Alice sends me out to represent our student government at another college. I have to give a little speech, which I hate. I feel stupid and it gets worse after my speech when one girl comes up to me and says, "That's the worst speech I ever heard in my life."

A sympathetic guy comes over to me. "Don't listen to that woman; she's the campus fool," he says. "She only repeats what everybody else says."

*

"I gave Professor Impellitiri your exam to grade," says the department chairman. "And no sooner did I give it to her than her father promptly dropped dead. So is it all right if I give it to Professor Kramer to grade?"

Kramer. That sadist. But I dare not object.

*

Alice and her boyfriend Richie see the art show on the Promenade. Alice feels constrained by Richie's presence and merely says hi to Mr. Blomberg.

This morning Alice was wondering what it would be like never to get married. She tells Ronna, "I couldn't imagine it."

In the beginning of their relationship, Alice wouldn't write things in her journal that might hurt Richie's feelings – even though he would never read them. But now she's being more honest with herself.

Today she wrote, "I've decided I would like a fling."

~ 123 ~

*

I tell Dr. McKenzie-Smith, "You know, I haven't been feeling that bad lately." She just smiles.

I ask her if she went to Martinique on her vacation. Later I realize why: because on Sunday I kissed a girl who had just come back from Martinique.

*

I buy some graduation cards, twenty-five cent ones for Joshua, Fay, and Sidney, and a thirty-five cent one for Ronna.

"You're playing favorites," the woman at the cash register tells me.

*

I am taking Professor Kramer's final in Mailer and Bellow. In the middle of it, I notice him taking out my comprehensive exam and reading it. He is chuckling to himself, the sadist. I've got to concentrate on my final, not on the exam he's grading.

*

At Ronna's house, the dog vomits in the living room.

Her brother, watching baseball on television, shouts, "The Houstons are winning!"

Fay and Alice call for Ronna. It is our third date, so we are skipping it and she is going out, she says, "for an evening with just the girls."

They go to a nightclub in the city. Everyone gets drunk except Ronna, who merely gets gas from drinking three ginger ales.

Coming home on the subway, a man exposes himself. "But don't worry," Ronna later tells me, "I didn't look."

*

I am amazed at the pure *dreck* I am putting down in my term papers.

*

I go out to Carvel to get a Happy 25th Anniversary cake for my parents. A lot of people get married on Memorial Day weekend. My parents, for one. And Ronna's parents would have been married twenty-four years today if they hadn't gotten divorced. My cousins Missy and Phil are having their seventh wedding anniversary but their divorce will become final soon. My old girlfriend, Dr. Field's old patient, has been married two years. I remember how proud I was the way I weathered the weekend of her wedding without too much trauma.

*

I finally go to the dentist. I have seventeen cavities, he tells me, "some of them major excavations."

*

I have a dream. I go over to Joshua's house to pick up a book and everyone shouts, "Surprise!" It is a surprise birthday party. Ronna gives me a big kiss. Everyone is there: Alice and Richie, Fay and her fiancée,

Dinnerstein and his girlfriend, Sidney, some of Joshua's degenerate friends, the whole crowd from school, and Ray Davies from The Kinks.

The best birthday of my life, and it's a dream.

*

Dr. McKenzie-Smith analyzes my dream. It is not hard to understand, she says. My birthday is next week and I want love. I did not give a party for my parents' 25th anniversary, Dr. McKenzie-Smith notes.

I always remember everybody's birthday, I tell her. But I never get as many cards as I send out.

"An accountant of the emotions," Dr. McKenzie-Smith says to me.

*

A surprise. Kramer liked my final. He told me it was "brilliant, just brilliant," when I meet him in the elevator. He says he is recommending me for graduation with distinction. He invites me to his office, offers me a drink.

"You look like a Scotch man," he tells me.

He thinks I'll make an excellent teacher and tells me to visit him in the future.

*

I have another dream. In this one, the chairman of the department tells me, "The sky's the limit." I don't need Dr. McKenzie-Smith to analyze this dream.

*

"I can't see myself getting into a long-term relationship," Joshua tells me as we walk along the Promenade. "I'm just out to get laid once in a while."

*

Another note from Ronna. Where does she get the time? "Prepare for future shock," this one says. "It's almost that time."

*

In the hallway at school I catch a whiff of a smell, a smell I remember. It is the same smell that the children's dining room of an upstate hotel had a dozen years ago.

*

My father phones me from a store.

"Listen," he says, "do you want a small color or a large black-and-white? I know these things should be a surprise, but we didn't know which one to get."

Which costs more? I ask him. It seems that the color set is more expensive.

"Black-and-white is fine with me," I tell my father.

*

Ronna cuts out the horoscope column from the newspaper. It has something about people born on my birthday. "Expect a year of intense personal experience and strong responses to whatever the environment provides," it says.

I think it's all bullshit, but I put the column in my memory drawer anyway.

*

It is my birthday. I go to school to find out my grades. The campus is nearly deserted. Workmen are setting up chairs outside for the graduation exercises.

I find I have gotten all A's. I am happy to hear it. In my happiness, I make only a half-stop at the stop sign. A cop pulls me over.

"Let me see your license, kid," he says. "If you have one."

He thinks I am too young to drive.

I hand him my license. It has my birth date on it so he can see it's my birthday.

"Okay, kid," the cop says. "Next time stop, willya?"

*

I have another appointment with Dr. McKenzie-Smith. She does not wish me a happy birthday but says instead, "You've always told yourself it doesn't matter because, deep down, it does."

You can't put anything over on her.

*

My parents ask if it's all right if we use their left-over 25th anniversary cake for my birthday cake.

"Why not?" I tell my parents. "It's no big deal."

Besides the black-and-white TV set from my parents, I receive other birthday presents.

Alice gives me a recorder, the kind we used to play when we were in second grade together.

Fay and her fiancé give me a box of banana-flavored stationery.

Joshua forgets to get me anything.

Sidney brings me some kind of antique and asks me to guess what it is.

"A pair of curling scissors?" I guess.

"Nope," Sidney says, "it's a candle snuffer."

Ronna gives me several things: a terrarium, *The Best Loved Poems of the American People*, and a furry frog. Also a card that says, "If you wake up on your birthday feeling like you've had it…be grateful!"

*

My father and mother, it turns out, were only joking about the cake.

*

~ 129 ~

Alice and I are reminiscing by her desk in the student government office. We drink a bottle of Cold Duck. We talk about our experiences at the college; then we talk about things way back.

I remind her of the time in second grade when our teacher wanted to show the class the size of a Canadian goose, which is four feet, the same height I was then. The teacher made me stand up in front of the class and she told the students, "Kevin is the exact height of a Canadian goose."

Alice tells me how the others girls in sixth grade used to laugh at her because she didn't have a training bra. Who knew?

The phone on Alice's desk rings. It is College Relations. It seems the local news wants to interview an open admissions graduate at commencement tomorrow.

We immediately think of Ronna; Alice begins making arrangements.

*

It is a very hot and sunny day.

It's early in the morning.

We are all lined up, outside the gates. I help Joshua when the zipper on his gown gets stuck. I have a master's thing on my own gown.

The procession takes a long time.

~ 130 ~

Filing in.

Alma Mater.

People's parents.

Speeches by distinguished alumni from the capital.

The college president, by the authority vested in him, declares us graduates.

Cameras.

Congratulations.

Asking people what they'll be doing. I'm going back for another master's degree.

That's it.

*

That evening I watch the whole thing on the local news. My black-and-white set plays beautifully. The interview with Ronna makes my heart pound. She is sounding so eloquent.

The news reporter says that the school is better off for having students like Ronna.

Ronna smiles in her gown. The camera shows her talking with her mother and little brother.

I do something I once Hubert Humphrey do during the 1968 Democratic convention. I go over to the TV set and kiss the image of Ronna on the screen.

I get a shock.

Plant Parenthood

Nick married Gudrun because she couldn't take a phone message properly. Gudrun had just arrived in America and was staying with Anne, who had been Nick's girlfriend when he was a college instructor and she was his student. By the time of Gudrun's arrival, Anne was seeing Dick, a vice president at Xerox, who was married and had four children, of whom the eldest and the youngest had cystic fibrosis. Anne was happily letting Gudrun stay with her in Palo Alto because she needed company; Dick was trying to get a divorce but had to stay with his wife through her midlife crisis; as a result, Anne was left alone much of the time.

One day Dick called Anne's house and Gudrun answered the phone. She wrote Anne a message but she had misheard Dick's name and wrote *Nick called*. When Anne got home from work, she called Nick, wondering what he could want, annoyed that he was trying to insinuate his way into her life once again. Nick didn't have the slightest idea of what Anne was talking about, and finally Anne realized that Gudrun took down the wrong name. Meanwhile, Nick was telling Anne that he was depressed because his ex-wife had just remarried; it was then that Anne came up with the idea that Nick should marry Gudrun.

Gudrun was an illegal alien and needed a resident visa. She was a communist, and that got her into trouble with the immigration authorities. Mostly Gudrun's problem was that she talked too much. She desperately wanted to stay in America although of course it was the most corrupt society on the globe. Anne had gotten her job as a governess but that was too boring. So Gudrun needed to marry.

Nick was enthusiastic about the idea. For one thing, this would give him another link with his old love Anne; for another, it would help his ego weather the remarriage of his ex-wife. It would also be an occasion to throw a nice party. Nick and Gudrun met a few times, smoked some hash, watched crime shows on television together. Finally they went to the lawyers and drew up a marriage contract. They did not want to be responsible for each other's debts.

And so they got married. Anne was Gudrun's maid of honor and Nick's former brother-in-law was his best man. Even Dick managed to escape his neurasthenic wife and clinging children to be present at the wedding. Everyone had a good time; everything was mellow. What pleased Nick most about his marriage was that it would prevent him from being trapped in some other marriage for at least two years.

Two years is the time Nick and Gudrun planned their marriage to last. Any divorce before that and the immigration officials were likely to look askance and not let the divorced wife remain in the country. Occasionally throughout the marriage, immigration officials popped in at a moment's notice. But they always appeared satisfied with Nick and Gudrun's living arrangements. The officials were impressed by the single bedroom and the one king-sized bed and they liked the coffeecake Gudrun usually prepared. Sometimes they came just for the coffeecake alone.

Throughout her married life Gudrun slept on the sofabed in the living room. She and Nick never attempted to consummate their marriage except once, and that time Nick wilted with the effects of too much liquor. They never talked about sex together although both had been fond of it in the past and remained fond of it with other people. Both of them had affairs; and always the sex took place outside their home. Nick and Gudrun liked the idea of living in a chaste house. They took pride in their home. They were especially fond of their plants. Nick and Gudrun treated all their plants like precocious children. When they got divorced, dividing up the plants was the most difficult aspect of the procedure.

The two years passed quickly for them. One day Gudrun saddened the immigration officials by telling them that she and her husband had irreconcilable differences and could not stay married very much longer. The immigration officials offered their sympathy, told her she would still be able to remain in America, and asked for another helping of the coffeecake which by then was the primary reason for their visits.

Gudrun got all the hanging plants and Nick got the potted ones. They had another party to celebrate their divorce decree when it became final. Nick enjoyed the party and the knowledge that he would once again be alone in his house. Gudrun had been an amiable housemate, but he had recently begun to find her a bit of a bore.

The divorce party lasted a day and a half. Nick's ex-wife and her husband came with their new baby and Nick publicly professed delight at his first glance of the boy he called his "reverse stepson." Gudrun was appalled by all babies and spent most of the party talking to Anne and to Dick, who was still in the process of trying to extricate himself from his suburban marriage.

"He wants to be Superman," Anne told Gudrun when they were alone. "He wants the divorce but only if everyone's happy. His wife has to keep the house and the car. The kids have to be able to keep going to Vassar and Hotchkiss. And I have to be..." Anne never finished this last sentence.

Gudrun looked at her old friend and smiled. "I wish I could arrange your life as well as you've arranged mine," she told Anne. Gudrun was deliriously happy when she was not pensive. She was involved in earthquake detection research and had in fact been part of the team which had correctly predicted a mild 3.8 quake just north of Bakersfield not three months before.

"Sometimes I think he'll never get divorced," Anne told Gudrun. "Dick is such a perfectionist. That's why I'm almost sorry he's here, seeing how perfect your divorce is and everything. He'll wait till he can have the perfect divorce too." She looked in Dick's direction and saw that he was dancing with Nick's former sister-in-law.

Gudrun scratched her eyebrow. For some reason she said to Anne, "Why don't you marry *Nick*?"

Anne closed her eyes at the words. "No. God, living with him was so *boring*. At least years ago, when I first went out with him, he could get me so angry that I once punched him in the nose. I would go out of my mind with boredom being married to Nick."

"And what should one expect? Nick *is* boring. But then so is Dick, I imagine." Gudrun looked over in Dick's direction and frowned.

"Do you have a lover?" Anne asked Gudrun.

"Yes, but he's mostly gay."

"That must be nice."

"Oh," said Gudrun, "it's all right. He makes excellent broccoli soup."

"Broccoli soup is good cold," Anne said.

"We like it hot better."

Anne nodded. Dick was coming over to her, holding the baby, the son of Nick's ex-wife. He would expect Anne to admire the child and whisper in his ear that she wanted to have his child. Dick's only son had died the year before of cystic fibrosis. The thought of having children nauseated Anne. She couldn't picture herself as a mother. Although she was approaching thirty, Anne's grandparents were all living and quite active.

Gudrun watched Anne watching Dick watching the child. She looked across the room and saw Nick and his ex-brother-in-law talking, probably about mutual funds. On the couch the baby's parents looked like they were having a fight; they were smiling altogether too much.

Gudrun said, "Excuse me," to Anne and Dick and hurried as discreetly as possible to the bedroom that she had supposedly shared for two years. The door closed behind her, she fell on the bed and started crying for no reason at all.

In two more minutes she was pulling the leaves from Nick's philodendron. Something about it had upset her.

Sex Stories for Teens

1.
Hugging.

I am hugging Kareem.

I am hugging Kareem because he is my best friend.

I am hugging Kareem because he has made law school.

I am hugging Kareem because I am so happy for him and because it feels like the thing to do.

Tina, another friend, is smiling as she watches me hug Kareem. She thinks: oh fuck, I don't see people hug like that enough.

Tina is seven months pregnant.

2.
Kareem's grandmother worked for rich people downtown. One night at a party, a man with red hair came into the master bedroom and raped her on the bed while all the coats were still on it. Kareem's grandmother did not cry out while he fucked her. She was only the maid. The man told Kareem's grandmother his name was Ray, like Ray Charles. Then he went back to the party. Kareem's mother was very light-skinned.

The man Kareem called his grandfather died when he was four. He lived mostly with his grandmother even then. His grandmother overprotected Kareem. Kareem was on the swimming team in high school and won a couple of medals, but to this day Kareem's grandmother insists he cannot swim.

3.
Tina and Kareem and I are driving in my car to the Slope, where Tina's obstetrician's office is. Tina is not sure she wants the baby. She got carried away at some party. I think she wishes she hadn't gone to that party, but now it is too late.

My care needs new shock absorbers but I can't afford them. Tina and Kareem and I feel every bump — especially Kareem, who sits in the back seat. He tells Tina she should sit in the back seat in her ninth month and I giggle. I have locked the seatbelt under Tina because it cannot go over her pregnant lap.

Kareem tells Tina that if she does not want the baby, he will take it and will raise it himself. Being a single father would not be that hard, Kareem thinks. He would do what his grandmother did.

"Fuck you," Tina tells Kareem.

4.
Many years ago Tina spent a night at her grandmother's house. That week her grandmother discovered a large

sum of money that she kept in the master bedroom was missing.

Tina's grandmother never accused her directly, but she implied to Tina's parents that Tina had stolen her savings. When her parents questioned her, Tina cried her eyes out. She never touched or took anything from there. But since Tina had slept over there and no one else did, everyone doubted her.

Two years after that, Tina's grandmother died at 81. Her mother asked Tina to attend the funeral, but with such a past, Tina just couldn't. Besides, she did not want her fucking family to know about the kind of life she was living.

5.

After her appointment with the obstetrician, Tina feels depressed. She has a bad headache. Kareem, who is still jubilant over making law school, says we should all drive down to Fulton's for ice cream sodas. I start to drive there. On the way there, Tina says she isn't at all hungry.

At Fulton's, I order a coffee ice cream soda. Kareem orders a black-and-white. Tina giggles and decides to order a strawberry float but barely touches it. I give her a Datril for her headache, but she says it does not do her any fucking good.

Afterwards we go to Kareem's apartment. It is Friday afternoon. We watch television and see a plane crash. Kareem takes Tina and hugs her. Then Kareem hugs me. Then I hug Tina, although not too tightly because

I am afraid I might hurt the baby. I think kissing her is okay.

Kareem asks Tina if she still has a headache.

"I can't remember," Tina says, "not with all this going on."

6.
When we are alone, Kareem says he bets that Tina's baby will be a real rapscallion. I laugh, but then I admit it.

"*Entre nous*," I say, "what the fuck is a rapscallion? A talking vegetable?"

"No, no," says Kareem. Now he is laughing. "It's a rascal, a rogue, a scamp. You've never heard the word?"

I shake my head no.

"I've known it since second grade," Kareem tells me. "It was a word in my reader in a story about a raccoon. When I came home and used the word, my grandmother said I was making it up, that there was no such word. It bummed me out that she didn't believe me."

Kareem looks wistful. *Wistful* is a word I hardly ever use.

"Oh, she didn't mean anything by it," I tell him, then wonder if that was a dumbfuck thing to say. "What does it matter? You're going to law school and you've got a big vocabulary."

"Not just a vocabulary," Kareem says, and the two of us start laughing like fucking idiots.

7.
I ask Tina why she doesn't try to find out if the baby will be a boy or a girl.

"It doesn't matter," she says, not really listening. "Either way I'm fucked."

Tina is thinking of when she was in a junior high school production of *The King and I*. She cried every night when the king died at the end of the play even though she was just a Siamese princess in the chorus. She also cried every time the king's head wife sang the song "Something Wonderful."

Tina is also thinking of writing a book called *Sex Stories for Teens*.

8.
Kareem calls me up to invite me to go ice-skating with him. I tell him I can't, that I have to write a paper for my English class on *carpe diem*.

"Oh," Kareem says. "The Vietnamese dictator."

Kareem knows how to make me laugh. "You know very well it means 'seize the day,'" I tell him. His vocabulary is huge.

"Right on," Kareem says. "I'll be over in ten minutes to pick you up. And be sure to have on a heavy sweater. It's fucking cold tonight."

9.

I met Kareem in high school. They transferred me there because the school needed more white students to get beat up. A bus took me there and picked me up. None of us white kids could drive but we wouldn't have known how to get to the school even if we could. We never looked out the bus window.

I used to get depressed because I was the only white boy in my official class. So I used to stay out of school. One time I stayed out of school two weeks and said I had colitis. But I was really wandering the subway system, eating donuts.

When I finally returned to school because my parents fucking made me, Kareem handed me a get-well card with a funny saying. This made me feel guilty because I hadn't really been sick.

I started coming to school more often and I started becoming Kareem's best friend. To this day he still thinks I had colitis. Every once in a while he says something about how good it is that I don't have it any more and I get uncomfortable.

But now there's no point in telling him the truth.

10.

I am half-Irish, like the man who raped Kareem's grandmother.

After we drink a pitcherful of beer, Tina tells me that she sometimes wishes that Kareem were the father of her baby. She says not to say anything, but sometimes she has fantasies about it. She and the baby could go to law school with Kareem and take care of him and laugh at his lame jokes.

I tell Tina to accept fucking reality. She asks me for another Datril.

11.

Months pass.

Tina has her little girl, and it is not too unhealthy. Tina goes home to live with her mother. The father of baby actually comes around one day and offers to marry Tina, but she never liked him and says no.

Kareem goes away to law school and I take over his apartment. He leads a pretty monastic life, he tells me, spending many hours in the law library briefing cases for class. Talking to Kareem and reading his letters aren't as good as seeing him in person. The last time we talked, he assured me that Tina's daughter will grow up to be a rapscallion.

I write Tina and Kareem that maybe all three of us (now all four, including the baby) can get together for Christmas. Tina writes that she is going to take the baby to Florida instead. They have both been ill and are tired and the warm weather will do them both a world of good. Kareem writes back that he wishes he could make it, but he has already accepted an invitation to spend the holidays with his new girlfriend from law school. He doesn't mention the girlfriend's name. Kareem says he will give me a call soon.

After I finish my schoolwork, I go to Fulton's and have a coffee ice cream soda. But it doesn't taste any fucking good. They must be using a cheaper kind of ice cream.

Richard Grayson is a retired lawyer and teacher who divides his time between Sunrise Golf Village, Florida; Apache Junction, Arizona; and Williamsburg, Brooklyn.

His previous books include *With Hitler in New York, Lincoln's Doctor's Dog, I Brake for Delmore Schwartz, I Survived Caracas Traffic, The Silicon Valley Diet, Highly Irregular Stories, And To Think That He Kissed Him on Lorimer Street* and *WRITE-IN: Diary of a Congressional Candidate in Florida's Fourth Congressional District.*

www.ingramcontent.com/pod-product-compliance
Lightning Source LLC
Chambersburg PA
CBHW050819180626
46814CB00004B/1366